THE MANY MINDS OF *ME*

A Book of Short Stories and Poems for The World, from My Mind.

KINGSLEY C. NURSE

So yeah, this is my *own* original work.
You can't use it without my permission.
Right? After all, I wrote the darn thing. Yeah?
To be safe, let's just throw the copyright in here.
I think it makes it look legit. **:.)**

Thanks:

To God, for giving me the words to express the thoughts of my mind.

And to Darolyn, whom I kept up late, many a night, forcing her to read my manuscript, word by word, story by story, poem by poem.

For:

My Precious Mother, whom, above all else, I wish could read what I wrote.

This Book is Dedicated:

To My Childhood and Yours. For there was a time, that nothing mattered more to me than going under a blanket, and getting absorbed in a good book. I often read from early afternoon until it got late, sometimes well into the night. This is for you, the inner child who once read, and continues to read nonstop, like the dickens.

Table of Contents

Foreword

Dear Reader,

I thank you sincerely and deeply, from the bottom of my heart, for taking a chance and looking at my book. This means so much more to me than any amount of money or fame, for it is the reader who brings the author's words to life; all in their amazing, imaginative minds.

I always wondered how an author would feel to know, long after posterity, that whole classes of students and adults or even strangers were reading their words, analyzing them, searching the meanings, and interpreting their thoughts.

Well, I can say, it is truly, and unequivocally, the *best* feeling in the world. You reading my words is as exciting to me as a kid waiting for Christmas morning to open their presents! I will never get over that feeling.

I hope you enjoy.

From my *mind* to yours,

-*Kingsley*

Part I

The Compelling Short Stories

"It was a dark and cold night. Leaves had strewn themselves all over the ground like a dirty blanket of paint, paint whose color appeared quite undesirable. Colors of paint that are horrible. A color of paint that you never pick. Horrible, ugly, disgusting paint. Tents were strategically placed around a large campfire that roared relentlessly. The fire roared nonstop. It was a strangely energetic fire. This fire seemed like it wasn't capable of being put out by man or beast. A fire that, if you dared venture too close you would be devoured but for the sheer monstrosity of it."

-From, *Midnight Camp Fire*

Introduction (The Compelling Short Stories)

Short Stories are amazing! They are truly my favorite. Give me a short story in prose over a long drawn out novel any day. With the format of the short story, you can think up one simple concept, and expand it out to make your point, all without relying on tens of thousands of words. The freedom of a short story is nigh unlimited. You can exemplify, to your heart's desire, a simple idea, a passing thought or a well-known, or even a lesser-known precept. Advantageous still, you can then later expand on this idea, growing it to great lengths if you so choose.

As for the short story, you have the freedom to describe it how you please! You don't have to keep in mind a relevant structure, or frame of sorts, meant to sustain the plot, not if you don't want to.

For me, the short story is meant to provide a lesson. A lesson the reader is rewarded with, after only a brief amount of time spent with your words. All you need do, is make it enticing enough for the reader to be just curious enough to want to read it. I love to entice a reader in, with the first few sentences of my story, and with the use of splendid epigraphs.

With the short story, you can quickly build the world and structure of your choice, and still leave out enough, such that the reader may use their imagination to fill in the message and obtain the "jewel" or crux of the story. You do not need a novel or a hundred thousand words to do this. This is one of the reasons why I love the short story.

Of course, you may do this to a greater extent with other longer forms of prose, and I may one day do this same above-mentioned thing, and expand on interesting concepts of my choosing, but this is not what I originally set out to do. I set out to share my ideas in short story form, and appreciate the short form of the work itself; for a novel to me, becomes tedious in identifying a plot, then casting a world around your protagonist, looking for, or perhaps creating conflict, then finally, to see it resolved.

Doing anything other than this is unfair to the reader, for they invested much time in reading some seventy to eighty thousand words. You must then, by the laws of "literary moral guidance and etiquette", provide a seemingly decent resolution to the conflict. But alas, why must a story have a resolution? Why must the conflict in the story end? To this, I say no. A story can be told with no ending in sight, no resolution of the conflict, no final conclusion to be had. You, the reader, may then superimpose your imagination to wonder or decide what the ending of the conflict may be. This is what I feel I am able to do with some of my short stories.

I also want to make the point in defense of the short story. It is important for you to know, that this type of short-form prose is just as genuine and realistic as any other; please do not let anyone tell you otherwise. If you endeavor to compose a short story, do so, for the world needs more; even in-spite of the herald of many who claim that the short story is not a desirable thing. Let me tell you. The short story is what shaped my imagination as a child. When you create a short story, you get to make a powerful point, and the reader remembers it forever. While I have forgotten most of the words from some of the other famous work I read as a child in novel form, I have never once forgotten a lesson I learned from a short story. Such is the power of this form. Thus I pray that I wield this power well.

In further defense of the short story, it is also wise to realize and be cognizant of the time a reader may want to invest in reading the work. Certainly, it is the reader's choice of how much time they choose to invest, but from the perspective of a busy adult, I have come to appreciate the value in reading a story meant to be contained in just as sufficient an amount of words you may read in one sitting or in the course of your break.

This type of brief storytelling is what is precious to me. I use it with all respect and adoration. As I coin the thoughts of my mind, the short story gives me just the space I need to parallel these thoughts to you. This, above all else, is why I love the freedom and structure of the short story. Did I mention how much I love the Short Story?

May you have as much fun reading my ideas, as I enjoyed writing them!

Midnight Camp Fire

"A Beacon of Hope, yet a Symbol of Fear, Doth help the frozen cope, or cause Man to shed the tear?"

It was a dark and cold night. Leaves had strewn themselves all over the ground like a dirty blanket of paint, paint whose color appeared quite undesirable. Colors of paint that are horrible. A color of paint that you *never* pick. Horrible, ugly, disgusting paint. Tents were strategically placed around a large campfire that roared relentlessly. The fire roared nonstop. It was a strangely energetic fire. This fire seemed like it wasn't capable of being put out by man or beast; a fire that, if you dared venture too close, you would be devoured but for the sheer *monstrosity* of it.

In the distance, the sound of many feet drew nearer. As the men approached, loud cries could be heard. Cries of power and of song; an increasing spectacle. As their leader approached the camp ahead of the men, he led the group, and the men following behind repeated his refrain: *"To follow is to lead, for honor, we will bleed!"*. They were a young group; men no older than twenty-five, and some as young as sixteen. As they entered the camp, they became louder and louder as if to match the intensity of the roaring fire. *"FOR HONOR WE WILL…"*

"Silence now my children, I must speak to you all."

"Yes."

"Tonight, is a very special night, a special night indeed. You are all chosen men."

"Yes."

The group of men answered in one accord. They always answered in one accord.

"You were chosen for a special purpose and now, my children, you are ready to know that purpose. But before I tell you this, you must prove to me, your leader, how devoted you are."

One of the older-lings spoke up. *"What can we do to prove it to you dear leader? We follow you day and night, and we would do anything for you. Tell us, how can we prove it?"*

The men listened intently. As the leader talked, the wind picked up and blew. It blew the flame to one side towards the men, and almost gave the appearance that it too, listened intently at the words of this great man.

"I will tell you. Is anyone here willing to bleed? Will you shed some of your blood for me? Me, your Great Leader?"

The men were *quick* to respond. Almost mechanically they shouted, *"This is our creed! For honor will we bleed!"*

The leader seemed extremely pleased. A satisfied smile came over his face. This smile was no ordinary smile. It was the smile of a king, nay, a Great Leader, a leader who knew that his men would follow him to fight, to war, to hope, to accomplishment, to death. As he stood there and looked at his men, he scanned over them with his eyes, once over, then twice, looking as if to scan for injured bruised whelps that were diseased and old, to pick out and eject the weak and tired, to embrace only the young and strong for his *noble* purpose. Satisfied with his survey, he turned and looked at the raging fire.

It was very late. It was approaching midnight. Now, the long-awaited answer finally came.

"I want you all to climb that tall tree over there and jump from it without hesitation."

The group of men seemed to become silent, almost instantly, for they knew nothing of the meaning of the thing that their leader had asked them to do.

After about what seemed like an *eternity* of about three minutes, a solemn, brave volunteer stepped forward and proclaimed he wasn't afraid and that he would go first. He said he trusted the leader and he knew that the leader wouldn't ask of them something he thought would harm them.

"And besides…" he thought, *"a fall from a tree may do me damage, but a jump can be controlled. I can make sure I jump feet first and let my feet take the brunt of the impact."* He thought briefly of what the jump would feel like on his poor legs, then stepped out and headed to the tall tree in the corner of the camp.

As the brave young man laid a hand on the lowest hanging branch of the tree, he wondered to himself if any of his campmates would follow. Quickly pushing feelings of loneliness aside, he began to climb. Climb and climb, he did, until he reached the very top of the tree. The tree at the top was a relatively decent height. The tree was about sixty feet tall, a tall one indeed. As the young man looked down on the ants below, he wondered how the tree had managed to grow taller than it appeared from the ground. Surely it had grown several feet further just during the God-forsaken climb alone.

One of the ants shouted out from way below.

"Are you going to jump?"

The leader stood apart from the rest, watching. Watching and smiling. His noble face somehow visible from the rest of the watching plebeians.

"Yes. Just hold on. Hold on"

"What are you waiting for? Do it."

At this point, impatient at seeing no bird fall from the heavens, they all shouted in unison:

"Do it, do it, do it!"

As the men shouted, the wind picked up again. The wind blew through the top of the tree and the top branches swayed back and forth, carrying the hesitant jumper. Smoke from the monstrous fire roaring still in the middle of the camp had ascended like a bird and reached the eyes of the young man. It stung. The unfortunate young man held tight to his branch like a buoy. As the young man looked at the faces below, something happened.

Something very strange.

Fear crept in and overtook his soul. He became terrified.

He was extremely terrified.

Terrified beyond belief.

Terrified at the thought of jumping.

Terrified at the thought of dying.

Terrified at the thought of dying in front of all those miserable ants so far below, and even embarrassed at his *"wisdom"* to venture first on this mission of devotion alone. This was all the young man could take; this was all the young man could bear.

As he held on tightly to a branch, he realized that he wasn't ready to die. He just wasn't. He had so much to live for, and he wanted to live it. And then, as the wind died down, the young man made up his mind.

He started down from the top of the tree.

As he climbed down the men shouted in disbelief.

"What happened? Why are you coming down? Are you scared?"

As he approached the ground, the young man looked over to the leader and thought he noticed a terrible expression of a scowl on his face, but as he got closer to the ground, the scowl seemed to change to a bright smile.

Finally, on the beloved ground, the young man walked up to the group of men with head hung low, ready for the remarks and insults he would receive.

"You coward!"

"You chicken!"

"What a scared little baby!"

"Pathetic little…"

He looked pathetic indeed.

Just then, the leader spoke.

"Silence children"

"Yes."

The leader spoke directly to the coward.

"Tell me, my child, were you scared? Were you scared to jump?"

"Yes leader"

"I see."

The dignified leader looked at the fire once more. The fire appeared to dance a little.

"Let me ask you again. Are you willing to shed blood for me now? Are you willing to die for me?"

The young man was not so quick and sharp as before. He slowly raised his head and said shamefully:

"I don't want to die."

The leader, to the great surprise of the group, laughed. He let out a strange laugh. A laugh of disrespected noblemen; haughty at the thought that such ill respect could be shown of subjects of his. He raised his brow and spoke, clearly and still...

"If you are not willing to do this for me, then you must leave."

The young man looked at the leader in shock. What? Was he being chased from the presence of his dear leader? Was the man he trusted so much, now shunning him, telling him he must go?

The young man opened his mouth as if to speak, to defend his cowardly action, but was severely cut off.

"If you cannot do this for me, then you must leave."

The leader repeated the ultimatum more strongly and firmly. The young man didn't know what to do. He looked at the camp. He looked at the fire. Oh, that burning pile of strength! If only he had the courage to burn with such veracity, such strength, such devotion. But unfortunately, he didn't. As the young man looked at his leader, he realized that this was impossible for him to do, impossible for him to achieve, impossible for him to carry out. He must leave the camp and go home. How painful and agonizing it must be for him!

The young man took one last look at the leader and proceeded to walk to his tent, with the group of men glaring at him. He packed his things silently and with a broken heart, left the camp.

The leader, noble and strong, paying no attention to the loss of one of his flock, cleared his throat and issued this warning:

"If you can't prove to me you are truly devoted, then you are not wanted here. You may leave now. You may leave just like that lost soul of a man."

At those words, there was a sound, a sound of the rustling of leaves.

Leaves like footsteps.

Footsteps towards Fate.

Fate sealing the Brave.

The Brave to *Destiny*. The Destiny of the tree.

The Destiny of obedience to their leader.

The young man, away from camp in the distance, could hear the sounds of screams in the night. *Surely*, they were screams of joy and laughter. Oh, what a terrible choice he had made! Walking in the distance, the young man could still see that roaring fire. The blaze glowing on, in the dark of the night.

Office Blues

"The World has two types of people inside. People who know they are not all there, and people who haven't gotten there yet."

Hey, so my name is Zacry. No, not Zachary. My mother said I looked like I was a "Zacry" when I was born. She cried. She said I seemed like I would make people cry. She was that sensitive. I mean, she *obviously* thought I would make people cry happy tears. All I know is that she didn't want people to confuse my name with Zachary or something else. She specifically wanted Zacry. Well, I don't think people would confuse it anyway.

I wanted to tell you about my life, but that's too boring. Who cares about someone's backstory? Instead, let me tell you that I like desks.

I remember looking at my first desk. It was so long ago. People never understood it. "Why do you feel such joy at looking at your desk?" They said. I always asked them how they didn't have the *same joy* as I did.

Honestly, sometimes, I feel as if this whole world has gone insane. No seriously. I feel as if everyone has gone crazy and I am the *only* sane person left alive.

I mean why not? Every single day I go to my office, and to my great dismay, my silly boss wants me to repeat the same things that I did the exact day before. What a friggin' idiot. I mean, who in their right mind does that?

Yet I do what he asks and repeat my work. He says I won't get paid if I don't.

What an idiot.

You would think the guy wants to change things up a bit? Seriously. But no.

Now don't get me wrong. I don't really care about my job, but I love my desk. I stare at it all day long. Staring is something I love to do. It is so comforting to me. I call it my *comfort* exercise.

Let me tell you. You caught me at a good time, and I'm kinda in a storytelling mood, so let me tell you about this one crazy guy I met at work the other day. He was an unusual fella; he smelled all clean and cut. I mean, the guy looked like he showered every day or something. His suit was all pressed and neat. I mean, who does that? What an idiot!

Anyways, I meet him in the elevator and I am doing my *comfort* exercises on the picture just behind his head and he looks at me and asks me what I wanted. I mean, why would he think I would want anything?

Well, I did the bigger man thing and ignored him and kept on doing my *comfort* exercises on the picture behind him.

At this point, I guess the idiot couldn't control his freakish desires for conflict and walks up to me and said I better stop staring at him or he would "bop" me in the nose.

Now what the hell was that about? I mean, sure he is an idiot, but why was he gonna "bop" me? I was pissed. But I kinda felt sorry for the guy and so I made up my mind to help him. Yes, help the poor bastard in any way I could. While he was talking to me, I could tell that the guy looked sleepy and tired, so I thought I would help him get some sleep.

I remembered I would buy these bird feeders as a boy and put sugar water in them. When a bird took residence in one, I would close the door and make him stay. They liked it. All my bird tenants did. They would fly around and bump their little head against every wall in their new house in gratitude. As they did so, they would chirp wildly. I was so excited! They would always ask me to let them stay forever and I told them the only way I knew how was to make them sleep with my special "*sleeping elixir*". To this, they chirped their approval. So as soon as I acquired a tenant, I would open a little hole in the box and pump in a little tiny bit of my sleep elixir through the hole. Man, oh man! They loved it! They loved it so much that they always fell to the ground and went *right* to sleep.

The only thing is, I had to stop making a home for these *sleepy* tenants, cuz' you know, they never wanted to wake up and leave. I had to stop buying feeders. Those tenants were gonna drain my little boy pockets!

Anyhow, back to the story.

I told him he better forget about bopping me because he looked tired. I told him I was willing to help him though. I told him I could make him sleep forever like my bird tenants and that all he needed was a little bit of my elixir.

Boy oh boy, was he mad! I mean, I didn't understand his anger. I was only suggesting a solution to his tiredness. I was actually only trying to help. At that point, he shoved me. He shoved me so hard! My back hit the elevator wall and to my great dismay, some of the sleeping elixir that I always kept on me in a little vial in case I saw a tired individual, fell out of my jacket pocket.

The idiot was determined to hurt me and steal my stuff. He asked me what it was that I had there.

Now, I am an honest chap, and it's a good thing I am. This one time, at the office, this lady came in, and I told her how she resembled and looked just as fat as a hippopotamus. I think she looked like one. I told her she did a good job of looking like one, and that she should keep it up. She seemed surprised. I think I pleasantly surprised her, and she seemed so happy, that she starting crying happy tears. She was probably really happy, as she was crying soo much!

She ran to the bathroom. I guess she didn't want to get her makeup messed up. The next day, I saw her walking in the office with another guy, and he walked up to my desk and told me that I should stay *away* from his "finances" or "financee" or something like that. Like I would mess with that guy's money or something. What an idiot!

Also, she never says anything to me anymore. Well, I don't think I helped her, because I see her drinking these cans of diet drink and I hear her mention she had a gym membership. She also said something about me being a crazy jerk. Why was "*I*" a crazy jerk? I only spoke the truth. Women. I tell you. They don't appreciate the truth. They seriously don't.

Ah well, back to my story.

I told the guy in the elevator that I had a little supply of *sleeping elixir* that I always kept on me, and that I would open it and give him a taste. Up to this day, I am still baffled at what he did next.

He ran to the other corner of the elevator and said I should stay away from him. I mean, he was the one shoving me and telling me he would "bop" my poor nose unless I stopped my *comfort* exercises.

How can you help people like this? This dude was literally crazy!

I sensed that this guy really needed my help, so I told him I would give him some of my *sleeping elixir*, and that he would be as good as rain. I walked up to him and he just cowered to the ground like I was gonna hurt him. Poor bastard.

Right when I got close enough to him to give him a little taste, the elevator door opened and he squirmed out of it like he was in danger. I yelled after him, but he kept saying I was crazy and that I should go to hell.

I mean, what a giant idiot. You really can't help people.

Later that day, some lady from human resources came up to my desk and interrupted my *comfort* exercises and asked me if I had "threatened" anyone earlier that day. I told them I hadn't, and that I was appalled that they thought I would. She said she wanted to search my desk and that I should let them before they called the cops.

Now, whoa! whoa! What did I do? I was starting to get pissed. This idiot lady was standing there and saying all these mean things to me and I didn't understand a bit of it. Anyways, I agreed for her to search my desk. I told her when she was done, she should apologize to me and that I would take her for dinner and drinks later.

She scowled at me and just started searching my desk. Now you see, I just don't get it. Why was she so upset? I was a perfectly nice guy and I didn't know why she made such a disgusted face.

Ah well.

After she searched my desk really good, she said it was clear, but that HR would be keeping an eye on me and that if I did anything like "that" again, I would be instantly fired.

I asked her what she meant by "that". "Did you mean me asking you to dinner?" I asked.

She looked at me for like five seconds and walked away without saying a word. *I guess somebody wasn't that hungry*, I thought as I sat back down to my desk to resume my *comfort* exercises.

When I was leaving for the day, my boss called me into his office and said I should take some time off. He said it would be good for me and that I should seek help. He said he would permanently let me go, but I had not done anything wrong to anyone so he wouldn't do that, but that I needed immediate help. I declined his offer, as I told him I felt fine and that he should try to help that crazy bastard that ran out the elevator on the other floor.

My boss was a nice guy, but truly an idiot. He said he "insisted" on my time away, and that he wasn't suggesting it, but that he *mandated* me to it. I smiled at him. I told him I would take the time off, but I really didn't need it, and that I would be ready for work as soon as he needed me again.

As I walked out of the office, I thought I heard him say "yeah sure you freak", but I think it was the radio I had heard playing while I was sitting in his office. The thing is, my boss must have hidden that radio well, cuz' for the life of me, I couldn't see it.

Ah well.

At home, I got some of that Chinese food I had left on the counter, sitting outside from last week, and as I was eating, I sat on my couch. All around my living room I had some new friends I had made. Some *bird tenants*, some *snakes*, and even a pet *cat* that was sleeping on my rug. All of them sleeping so peacefully. Boy, did they love to sleep! I kinda wanted to wake them up, but they looked so peaceful. They had requested I give them some of my sleep elixir cuz' they looked tired. Being the generous guy that I was, I did. *No* other guy I know is more generous, I'll tell you that much.

I heard one of the snakes say as he was falling asleep that I should take some of it as well, as it would allow me to sleep too, but I told him, maybe later. Besides, I wasn't sleepy. In fact, I hadn't slept in like seven days or something. I must have a lot of energy. I think I'm the perfect specimen. Talent and good genes are what it is.

Anyways, I am here at home, waiting to go back to work. I suspect soon though. In any case, I looked for a picture of the HR lady that searched my desk earlier in the day. I looked it up on my computer. She was our company's HR manager. Her name was Paulette. Found her address too. Huh, didn't know it was this easy. I might look up several of the ladies who work with me in the office, maybe visit them sometime. They would be so happy to be surprised at home! Maybe I can come at two in the morning. How amazing is that? Maybe sneak in through a window and go all the way to her bedroom. They would say that it was the best surprise ever! Why didn't I think of this earlier?

After I ate, I decided I would do some *comfort* exercises next to the picture of the HR manager in my room, so I did. Shortly after I started, I got a call from my Aunt. I didn't answer my phone. I didn't like talking to her too often. She left a message asking me if I had taken all of my meds. She was cute. She *actually* believed I was taking medicine as a boy. *Jokes on her.* My house tenant friends told me that it was just candy, a long time ago and that I should stop eating it cuz it was just vitamins that I didn't need anyway. I would believe my bird and snake friends over her any day. She was always talking about the white rock candy I chewed on as a boy. My school nurse gave it to me *a lot* for some reason.

Well, I had grown tired of that candy, so I stopped eating it. She went on in the message about how I shouldn't ever forget to eat my candy. I got a little annoyed and I turned off my phone. I mean come on, I'm a grown man now. I don't need to eat candy anymore. I started to wonder if my Aunt was an idiot.

My Mother

"There is simply no way to quantify the love of the sole female who carried you. Don't bother to compare it with anything else. This is a special gift, given to us by God Himself. A remnant parallel, to the love he has for us."

She had passed about one year earlier. It's surprising because I don't remember exactly how I felt. I could go back to see, but that would be a waste of precious time. For me, the days were all a blur. I wasn't allowed to go to the exact moment of her death, but I was able to go to the exact time and date of the night before she passed. This, I was allowed to do, and I went back.

As you now know, I had gained the ability to travel through time with restrictions, but I was able to do so, undetected or noticed by anyone.

I traveled back to the night before she passed. She was sleeping soundly for the last few days without waking up.

As I walked into her room, the lights were low, and the room was dark, despite the small night light my father kept in the room to comfort her. She was tired. She had stopped eating several days before, and the first time my father called me to tell me, I somewhat dismissed it, as I felt that she would be sick from time to time and that sick people just don't have great appetites. So, I didn't feel like it was serious. But this time, it was.

My father was asleep in the large chair they place in the room for company to stay. He is also an old man, and as much as he tries to take care of things, it wears him out. I truly respect him for staying at my mother's side. '*Till death do you part* indeed, and he fulfilled that promise splendidly. Of course, things weren't always good for them, and they had many problems throughout the years, but he did the right thing in the end.

Indeed, as much as a good man can.

I remembered walking out of her room a year or so before that, and I had the weird feeling it would be the last time I would see her alive. In fact, it was, and if I didn't have this ability, it would have been.

I walked up to her bed. She was sleeping soundly. It was hard for her to sleep during the night on these last few days. A few nights prior, she had a very rough night, and the next day when my father came in to see her, he comforted her and told her that she shouldn't be afraid to die. This is true. You see, for we are Christian people, and we believe in Jesus and a future resurrection. This comforted my mother, and after this, she was able to sleep soundly.

As I stood there, I wondered and thought back to all the times I had been mean to her. All the times I hadn't listened to her. It broke my heart. She was already dead. Yes, not here at this present moment, but when I go back to my time, she *is* already gone. There is nothing I could do to stop this. The rules were clear. I was not allowed to interfere or interact in the past or the future. If I violated these rules, I would be wiped out of my timeline. I dared not do anything that I was told I could not do.

As I stood there, I wanted to cry. I wanted to wake her up and try to talk to her. I wanted to say my goodbye's. Alas, I could not. I walked back out of the room. My heart ached. I wanted to see her while she was healthy again. I wanted to see her when she was active and walking around. She had such a beautiful smile and was very photogenic. She was also very beautiful when she was younger.

* * * * *

Since I could travel through time to specific events I chose, and witness the events undetected, I went back to the most recent time we talked over the phone when she was healthy. She was always happy for me and very interested in what I was doing. She was always so excited to talk to me and my girlfriend when we called. This made me sad too, as I often didn't call her nearly as much. Well, as much as she wanted.

Give me one or two seconds of new time with her. I would trade days, no weeks, even months *off my life* to get a new minute with her now. But this is life. How strange we all are to neglect our family members while they are alive. Our loved ones. We sure are silly beings. If you're reading this, my dear friend, take a lesson from this one concept, do not neglect your family. Especially not your mother. Even if they are annoying to you sometimes. You will regret it if you can no longer speak to them again. Especially so, your precious mother.

At that moment when she was talking to me, I listened intently, as she asked me all the things that were going on with me. This was painful to see again, knowing I would hang up the phone and not talk again for a few weeks, but I resigned myself to experience through it. It was nice to hear her healthy voice. This I felt was a great gift, despite how I was feeling now, for no one else has been allowed to do this. Not to my knowledge at least. Since I could do nothing more than listen, I just cherished the sound of her voice, then left that moment in time.

Here is another lesson. Make videos of your loved ones. Keep them safe, tucked away. One day, you will long to hear and see them.

* * * * *

I visited a moment in time when she was crying. No one knows about this, as I was the only one to discover her crying at that moment. My family had tried to run a small store, but the business was failing. We were kids, so we couldn't help out in the way that would make the business prosper. We made it worse, as my parents had to ensure we had enough to eat while still trying to sell enough supplies to make a profit and put it back into the store. Ultimately, it couldn't last.

One day I came downstairs early that morning, and she was standing in the store, crying. What she told me I will keep to myself, but I understood even then what she meant. She was so sad. I wished at the time, that I was rich, and that I could give her all the money I had. I left that moment directly after she talked to me, as it was again, too painful.

Things of course got better, as there was a time in her life that I gave her whatever she asked. I had a lot of money, and if she called me and asked me for something, I practically gave her double. This was the least I could do for her. I wish I could have given even more. Had she not gotten sick and stayed well, I would have continued giving her *anything she wanted*, and all that I had.

* * * * *

There was a time when as a teenage boy, I was stupid and prideful and boastful. I will never, ever forget the sacrifice and care my mother had for me. She went out of her way to save me from embarrassment and shame.

You see, I had promised to raise a certain amount of money for my church. Once a year, my church had an event called Ingathering, where you go out into the community and essentially, ask for charitable donations or money for the church. I was a young teenage boy, and I wanted to out-do the adults. I had, in my pride and nonsense, promised that I would raise ten thousand dollars before the event was over. At that time, that was a large amount for a young boy to raise. Everyone was shocked. "No way you can raise that." they said. They were right. I couldn't. Not as a boy. Not at that time.

However, I was determined. I went out at the beginning of the event and started my charitable campaign. I knocked on doors all over. I was doing the footwork. I was going to school in the next town over, so I went there and knocked on the doors of the people in that community too. I was chugging along. I raised a thousand dollars easily. Two thousand dollars came quickly. Three thousand? A piece of cake. I got to four thousand and I was thinking to myself, sure, it's slowing down, but no problem. As I slowly got to five thousand dollars, I started to realize I was running out of people to ask for money. I had exhausted all the people I knew. I had exhausted all my neighbors who were willing to give. All the people I knew, *even some I didn't*. Remember, I was still a boy knocking on strangers' doors, in not well-known neighborhoods to me, asking for money. I worked hard for another few weeks or so, as the charitable event lasted several weeks. As it was coming to the near end of the final week, I hit my limit. I had raised a total sum of a little over six thousand dollars.

To some, this might seem good. You put in a good effort, *didn't you?* You raised over six thousand dollars. But for me, this was inadequate and embarrassing. I had spoken too pridefully, and I had boasted too much. I became very depressed and despondent. The church was calling for all the people to submit the final amounts they had raised. They had been calling for it since the first week, but they ask for the final amount at the end of the last week. I only had the six thousand dollars I raised, and I was ashamed to go to church, where there were people who I knew were just spiteful enough to laugh at me. Yes, laugh at a boy who promised ten thousand, but only produced six thousand. There were people like that in my church. I didn't want to be laughed at.

As the day came closer, I knew I had essentially failed. The day before the final day of the ingathering event, I decided I would not go to church. I set the money I had raised on my shelf and despondently said I wouldn't go, as I didn't have the amount I promised, and then went to bed.

The next day, the rest of my family got up and went to church. My mother came to my room and asked me if I was going. I told her I wouldn't go. She then asked me for the money to take it to church, as it was the final day. I gave her what I had and went back to bed.

After church, my family came home, and my parents didn't say anything to me, but I assumed I was laughed at by some, and others probably gave me the *"well he tried"* speech, but secretly smirked in their hearts.

When my brother got home from church, I asked him what happened. My brother told me.

I had promised ten thousand dollars. I had only raised a little over six thousand. However, when they took the envelope from my mother, they opened it up and counted up the sum of all the money in the envelope, and to everyone's surprise, it was exactly ten thousand dollars. People couldn't believe it. My then-girlfriend at church at the time told me that she just kept shaking her head in amazement at how I did it. Everyone was shocked. *"He did what he said! He raised ten thousand dollars!"* Only two other adults had done this besides me. As a matter of fact, they actually raised the same amount to match me, so as not to be outdone. Outdone by the boy who promised too much. Interesting how adults become competitive with children sometimes.

People were amazed, for the church saw ten thousand dollars delivered, and attributed the praise to me, and how I kept my promise, but I knew what had happened. You see, my kind mother, unbeknownst to me, had added the difference to the sum of money in the envelope, and even though we were poor and needed the money. She added the extra amount, close to four thousand dollars, to make up the full ten thousand.

My mother did that. All to save me from embarrassment and shame.

I will never forget what she did. No, not till I die.

* * * * *

My mother helped me to be what I am now. I didn't have money to go to a program I wanted to attend. She was working at the time to take care of the whole family, all by herself. We needed every cent to pay the bills, so she worked extra shifts just to give me the money to pay for the program. She gave it to me without any ask or thought of me returning it. She just wanted me to do well. I ended up doing very well and went on to make a six-figure salary because of her. I made sure I took every opportunity to let her know that it was because of her sacrifice, that I was successful.

* * * * *

One time, as a small boy, I was sick. I had stayed home from school, and my brother was two years younger than me, and he stayed home with me as well. I remember I was so weak; I couldn't get up out of bed.

As I lay in bed, I was feeling shorter and shorter of breath. I dozed off to sleep, and the next thing I knew, I was unable to breathe. I knew it was getting dangerous, even as a little boy, so I struggled and got up, and went to my mother's room which was next to mine. She was sitting on the bed, and I think she had just finished eating her breakfast. I remember walking straight to her and lying across her stomach, and I laugh a little now, as I remember her complaining to me that she had just eaten some food and that it was uncomfortable for her, and to get off her stomach.

I was barely able to tell her that I couldn't breathe. I then began to feel myself fading as my throat closed up. I was about to lose consciousness, but I could still hear and see a little. I remember her calling my brother into the room in a hurry, and she told him to run to the kitchen and grab something in the cabinet. In those days, my mother kept medicine in the kitchen cabinet. Nowadays, it's probably best to lock medicine away in the bathroom or a designated storage area. You don't want little kids able to access medicine so easily if you're not around. However, as kids, we seldom played around with strange bottles we didn't know about.

I remember my brother arriving back into the room with the thing she asked for. Looking back, it was probably Benadryl or something. She poured some of the stuff in a capful and gave me to drink. I still had a little consciousness and lifted my head and drank it. Immediately, my throat opened up and I could breathe again.

I think I had eaten something and was having a dangerous allergic reaction to it.

She saved my life that day.

* * * * *

Once there was a fire in our building. A family had moved into the building and their kids were messing around with electronics and old busted TV's and one of the kids sparked some wires and started a fire a few stories under us. They, of course, fled the apartment building without even an alarm or trying to notify any other people living above them. How nice of them. They were really wonderful people.

At the time, we lived on the fifth floor of the walkup. I still remember the address. I had come home from school early that day, and at the time, my grandmother on my mother's side lived with us. My youngest brother was home with my mother as he was still a child, and not old enough to go to school yet.

I remember coming home and taking off my sneakers. I was in the living room when the smoke detectors started going off in the house. My mother came out of the kitchen. She was preparing for dinner. She started looking around and saw smoke rising out the window.

She immediately sprung into action. She screamed for me to go put on my shoes right away. Startled by this, I didn't listen right away and ran to see what she was doing and what was happening. I saw my mother run to the front door and open it, and in one swoop, dash outside into the hallway.

She was instantly enveloped in thick, black smoke. She dashed back inside in the next second. The motion she took happened in an instant. To give you an idea of the speed she displayed, she was out the door and inside in literally two seconds.

She ran down the hall and got my grandmother, and my little brother, and rushed to get them ready. She took a glance at me, standing there like a fool, and she yelled at me again to go put on my shoes and go to the living room. I was shocked at what was going on, so I didn't listen and went to the living room to wait on her.

As she burst into the room with my little brother and my grandmother, she opened the front window. We were indeed fortunate, for we lived in a building with a front fire escape, and the fire was spreading towards the back. As she opened the front living room window, I remember feeling anticipation, that I didn't want to climb out the window, and that I didn't want to leave. But by that time, we knew danger was fast approaching, and the urgency of leaving was expedient. My mother opened the window and beckoned me first to climb out. I did and immediately looked down the five stories below. Not nice for a kid, I tell you that much.

She climbed out with my little brother and then helped her mother onto the shaky platform. People had now gathered outside across the street from the building to voyeur expectantly, excited to see people emerge from the approaching smoke. At this time, the fire trucks had begun to show up.

The smoke was steadily increasing and enveloping the air around us. At first, we all stood on the platform, a bit dazed and confused, standing there, so high in the air, watching people watch us. Smoke began burning our eyes. Suddenly, my mother beckoned me to come closer and told me to start making my way down the stairs.

I looked at her at first, wondering about what she had asked me, as I didn't want to leave them, but by this time, I knew the danger in the whole situation and knew that I needed to listen obediently. I started making my way down the stairs. As I got close to the fourth floor, I remember looking up once and saw my mother, my brother, and grandmother standing above me. My mother then shouted at me to keep going down the stairs.

After this, my memory remains unclear. For some reason, this moment in time was a "seminal event" in my life, and as such, I was not allowed to visit it again. I will present to you then, two accounts, one from myself, and one of which my mother, of which she told me afterward. I truly do not remember it as she told me, but I knew all too well that what she told me must be true.

My account is this: As I made my way down, past the fourth floor, a large waft of smoke blew towards me and enveloped me for about thirty seconds. As it burned my eyes, I remembered that I stopped and waited, because I couldn't see, and I waited to start walking again. Then I proceeded to walk down the stairs until it happened again on the third floor. This time, I held onto the rail of the fire escape and bent my head because the smoke was burning the hell out of me and I couldn't breathe properly. Finally, I made it to the first floor, where the firemen were waiting for me, and they pulled the first-floor ladder that hangs above the street down enough to the ground, and they picked me off the ladder and they told me to run across the street and go where everyone else was standing. This is my account of how I remember it.

My mother said it happened much, much differently.

My mother's account is this: As I approached the fourth floor, she said I started walking back towards her, and she had to yell at me to keep going. She said I then listened and kept going down the stairs. She then said that when I got to the fourth-floor platform, a large cloud of smoke blew towards me and I stopped walking. She then said that as I tried to turn away from the smoke, and it was burning my eyes and I was enveloped in the smoke and I couldn't breathe, that I panicked, and attempted to jump over the rails. She said as I placed my leg over the railing, she had to shout to me twice not to jump. She said she kept telling me not to panic and to just keep walking down. She said I listened to her voice and put my leg back inside the railing. She said it happened again to me on the third floor, and once again she had to shout at me not to jump. She said that I finally made it to the first-floor platform, and the firemen took me off the ladder.

I honestly can't remember what account was true. Did I panic and was trying to jump from four stories in the air? I honestly can't remember it happening that way, but I do believe that my mother would not have lied to me, so perhaps the true memory of what I experienced, I repressed. This is probably why I am not allowed to visit that moment again.

What I do remember though, was that I was barefoot, because I didn't listen to my mother to put on my shoes, and I had to walk on the ground, amidst all the broken cubes of glass. I surprisingly didn't get cut though.

My sister was walking home from school when she came upon the scene and found me standing outside. We stood there and looked up because my mother, my little brother, and my grandmother were still standing there on the fifth-floor fire escape platform. By this time, the smoke was getting intense.

The firemen did their job. They came up the fire escape but realized that my mother could not climb down safely with her mother, who was also beginning to be elderly, while also making sure my little brother was safe. They quickly extended the ladder with the cage at the top, to the fifth floor, and put my mother, brother, and grandmother inside. Then they descended slowly to the ground.

They were then put in an ambulance and whisked away to the nearby hospital for a checkup. They had been standing there for a good amount of time on the fire escape platform in the smoke, and the firemen wanted to make sure they didn't suffer from smoke inhalation poisoning or burns in their lungs.

Our family was spared, and we were saved. Saved by God giving my Mother the wherewithal to act in a dangerous situation. Saved by the quick thinking of my Mother.

* * * * *

The last moment in time I went back and visited with her while she was alive, was when I was again, a little boy. She had gotten up early and had kneeled to pray. It was an early morning, and I think I had a nightmare and I left my room and went into her room. I remember holding onto her as she knelt in the bed. I stood there, in the dark sleepy room, quietly, as she prayed. I wonder what she was praying about. Of course, God knows.

I went back to that moment, and watched, as I stood there as a little boy, silently at the side of the bed as she prayed, holding onto her. She always prayed. It wasn't easy over the years. But she got up every day and went to work to take care of her family. Her job was very tough. As she was rising to finish, I left the moment, as this was too painful to stay. I couldn't take it anymore, so I came back to my present time.

* * * * *

I know I will see her again. As for now, I am only allowed to go back and experience those few, precious moments in time. It is extremely painful, yet one may assume it is a gift, but the pain you experience in going back to witness your loved one, all while not being able to affect an influence on the timeline to motivate a single atom to move differently, is truly hard, and very excruciating.

It is somewhat like a playing movie, and you are the actor in the center of it all, playing out the events as it happened. The machinations of this affects you emotionally. It simply breaks your heart.

I am now back in my time. As I sit here thinking about this, I am staring at the clock in my bedroom, watching the seconds tick by. Strange how we use a clock to represent the forward movement of time. Looking at the clock's hands, I have come to understand more than most, the meaning behind each tick. Many thus wish the hands to rewind backward. But for me, I only wish to see it move forward. As quickly as possible. As far as I'm concerned, the ticks are *too slow*. I watch, as each tick takes its designed action, just as slow as the last one, ticking away in *slowness*. Ticking forward, but never reaching the future I wish to be in.

I can't wait till the day I get to see her again. Each tick forward on the clock brings me closer to this.

Time will ultimately move forward, and the future we look forward to, will one day be the present. For now, I must wait. We all must wait.

Years, Months, Days.

Hours, Minutes, Seconds.

For me, the infinitesimal time between the seconds are excruciating. I deeply lament this, for the second, while it ticks forward; it simply doesn't tick forward *fast enough*.

The Black Awakening

"It is time to Wake up, I say. Time to wake up, observe our surroundings, and really see. Truly see what has happened to us. What is still happening to us. Let us see what is become of us, then, let us fix it."

One day, in the future, the *Black race* woke up. They had had enough.

It was as if they were sleeping the whole time. Racism, drugs, violence, low self-worth, injustice, incarceration, unjust police shootings and killings, violation of rights, all of it. They decided enough was enough and decided to do something about the state and condition of Black people the world over.

This realization occurred simultaneously in all races and ethnicities of Black people. African, British, American, Australian, all Black ethnicities, and cultures. From the Black people living in England to the Black Muslims living in Egypt. This single realization began to permeate in their minds.

They simply had enough.

A society was formed. A Black representative from every culture and relevant location was chosen and represented. The nature of this society was solely to decide how and what should be done, and the next steps that should be taken. The Black race would then follow the directives and mandates of the council. This was unanimously decided the world over.

The Black men and women chosen for this council were from different walks of life, from different cultures and backgrounds. They were chosen for their high intelligence, their adaptability, their character, and their integrity.

Thus, the *Black Council* was thus formed.

Now, meetings began to be held. These meetings, once in session, held no ill intent. They were not designed to push or motivate any form of bad will, or recommend evil or trouble of any kind. The council was not racist by definition either. Care was taken to focus on doing everything with inclusiveness and mindfulness of other cultures, religions, and ethnicities. All cultures, creeds, religions, and ways of life would be honored and respected. It was even decided, that if other cultures and races chose to join in, the numbers and alliances would be greatly welcomed and deeply appreciated, for they knew and respected the old proverb, *"no man is an island"*. They knew they could not do it alone. They knew it would require any and all help offered and given.

At the opening of every meeting, the representatives all prayed. They prayed to their individual religious deities, and whom they believed their higher power was. They prayed for power, for victory, for life and for success in their objectives.

After many meetings, it was decided that Black people would rise above their plight. They would endeavor to elevate the status of the race to what it once was, or even *greater still*, to what it *could* be. They would help improve the world, all while helping to improve it for other downtrodden races as well. For this to happen, Black people would first need a few things, and as such, it was decided that it would be done through a series of steps.

Much deliberation went into how to go about the goals the council had set, and it was decided that there would need to be first, characteristics showed forth by all Black people the world over. There could be no success without these characteristics. The characteristics chosen were: *Focus, Selflessness, Determination, Kindness with Forbearance, and Patience.*

These characteristics were decided specifically, as the council knew that resistance would come to oppose the good thing they were trying to achieve. They knew it would not be easy, but if they were going to achieve this goal, they needed all Black people over the world to aspire to exhibit these five traits. They needed all to rise above the fray. Above the conscious and racial din. Above all the negativity. The five traits were explained as such:

Focus: Focus to keep to the task. There would be many distractions. Many, many distractions and temptations. It was determined that once the objective came out what they were trying to do, there would be those, even from their race, who would seek to distract and lead others away from the single purpose of elevating the Black community.

Selflessness: Selflessness would also be needed. This effort was a monumental task, and as such, massive resources, nay, vast resources would be needed. Some would have little to none, and those with plenty *must* be willing to share and pool their resources to help those with little. They must rise together, *or not at all.* Greed must be forgotten, and any success must be shared altogether, amongst the race. No matter how little or big the success was, no matter the monetary gifts you had thus prior obtained.

Determination: Determination to persevere through troubling, difficult times, of which there would be plenty. They knew that many Blacks would suffer through this huge undertaking, and as such, determination and perseverance was a character trait that must be developed and practiced.

Kindness with forbearance: This was meant to allow Black people to see each other and be willing to help. But none such that they only helped their race alone. This was a kindness to see *all races,* all people, and understand hatred. This must be combined with *forbearance* to walk away from violent, dangerous encounters. Forbearance to *refrain* from looting and rioting once socially or morally wronged. Kindness and Forbearance to exhibit mercy on those who wronged you. Kindness to turn the other cheek. This would be something the race would struggle with, as there seemed to be a lack of mercy, especially amongst their race towards each other. There were many now who would rather see their own dead, before seeing them succeed. This must be changed. A special effort would be made to ensure this trait was especially adhered to, no matter what.

Patience: Patience to understand and know that this change cannot happen overnight. Patient to know that many will fail. Many will struggle. Many will die. Many will face their demons and overcome them. Many will face their demons and be pulled to hell. Thus, there must be patience to understand, that a long game must be played. Just as those cruel forces played the long game to keep Black people downtrodden, they must now play the long game to rise above it. Patience would be needed to achieve this. *Indeed,* great patience.

Once those traits were published and spread to all Black people, it then came time to enact the anticipated plan. The plan to raise Black people out of the state of affairs they were presently in. It was now time for a call towards action. This must be a united front. This must be something all Black people must be willing to do and abide by. This first step came to be simply known as,

The Race Name Consolidation.

* * * * *

The Race Name Consolidation

As Blacks the whole world over began to interact in public, a strange thing was happening. No one knew how it started, or where it came from at first. All Black people, when referred to anything else other than *"African Black"* did not respond, but requested to be called as such before further discourse could be entertained. This took place in the news, in all forms of media; Newspapers, Television, Radio, Print magazines. Pretty much, *everywhere.*

Many interviews took a strange turn. When in the middle of a question about sports, or leisure, or entertainment, or anything Black people were inquired of, the interviewee asked to be referred to only as African Black, not African American or Black Canadian or any other designations of Black. It was largely ignored at first, with a few articles here and there pondering the strange choice of preference at first. But then, the fullness of the media finally caught on. They would ask every Black person why they only wanted to be referred to as "*African Black*". How could you be *African Black*, if you were born in New Zealand or you lived in Italy all your life? Surely *ALL* Black people don't want to be referred to as *African Black*? Further, what if you are of mixed descent?

The answer given was simple. Black people all over the world now, first and foremost only wanted to be referred to as *African Black people*. The rules were simple. If you could be genetically identified as of African descent, being that Black people are generally believed to be originated from Africa, they would only like to be referred to and identified as *African Black* going forward.

The articulate ones among them argued that this was necessary to have the world associate all people of genetic African Heritage as *African Black*, just as all people genetically identified as Italian are respectfully *referred* to as Italian, even if they live in America, Canada, or Europe. Same as for other races of people of various genetic descent.

The world was shocked at first because now *ALL* Black people took on the single racial identifier as *African Black*. It did not matter your culture. Nor your background. It didn't matter where you were born or where you came from, or where you lived.

You were born in Australia? You are to be referred to as *African Black*. Lived most of your life in Greenland with an Austrian mother and African father? You were *African Black*. Born in Russia or lived your whole life in the Netherlands? Still, *African Black*. As long as you genetically identified as having African Heritage and genes, you were *African Black*.

The media was flummoxed. Who decided this? And still more curious, how did *all* Black people decide to follow this one precedent, seemingly overnight? Discussion panels started taking up the subject. Large arguments and debates over the rightness or wrongness of the name often took place. Some scholars even began debating the authenticity of the age-old belief that Black people even came from and originated from the African continent. They posited that African people may have descended from a genetically deviant mutation passed down from the Neanderthals.

Indeed, now that all Black people wanted to claim Africa as their sole origin, many wanted to thus deny this as plausible. Many were amused and delighted at how fickle human psychology and interpretation was.

Prominent people lost their jobs and credibility as they boldly declared that they would never register their child's race as such, and refused to acknowledge their adopted Black child as *African Black*, and the rest of the proper "woke" media began to criticize and chastise them for it. It became such a huge deal, as the new idea dominated the news cycle for weeks, that the UN itself took up a resolution that this should be honored, and that no matter what your culture or creed was, as long as you were genetically identified as of African Heritage, you were to be referred to as *African Black* in all nations, and all languages.

Success.

Black people had managed to change their racial name and solidify their geographically accepted origin, and how they were referred to in the public and the world. They were now one completely defined race. This was a crucial step, one that seemed small at first, but was a very important detail that must be worked out. All Black people the world over were to be seen as originating from Africa, and not to be referred or attributed to any other physical country besides Africa, no matter where you lived. This was important, as now all Black people had established that they were one existing race, one group of humans who were to be treated as any other race. Unbeknownst to Black people at the time, this was to be an important aspect and driver of their *future* decisions.

Upon seeing this first success, the council of Blacks was encouraged, for this was relatively easy. No major bloodshed had occurred in this endeavor; no immense resistance to this concept. All Black people were happily referring to themselves as *African Black*, and all was so far, good.

It was decided then, that the next step of the plan should now be enacted.

Black people would now seek to brighten the realms of their minds. Black people would now seek as an entire race, high and low, rich and poor, to do something powerful, something that they never *wholesale* have done. Something necessary to beat back the tides of ignorance and injustice. Something to enlighten their minds, and bring them that much closer to their goal. They would gain their *Education*.

* * * * *

The Education Initiative

Blacks, or now known specifically as *African Blacks*, all over the world began to take their Education and learning seriously. I mean, *very seriously*. You could find Black people studying everywhere, spending any free time they had in Libraries, Book Stores, and Educational seminars. They went back to school. Single Black women started taking online classes and working towards their degrees. Black men from all over, who were so far, still uneducated, began to learn proper science subjects, and began to memorize relevant political vocabulary and discourse, and began to speak with proper language, even in the streets.

The use of the word *"Nigger"* was completely banned in all forms or representations of the word, whether in entertainment or otherwise. With it, banned words also included: *Nigga, My Nig*, or any representation or appropriation to it, and eliminated from the tongues and language of all Black people all over the world. It was never spoken or used by Black people to reference themselves ever again.

Not once more. Ever.

They also immediately stopped using phrases and words such as *Uncle Tom, Sellout, Simp,* or *Rat.* They also heavily discouraged the use of words such as *Snitch* and downright banned any other type of nouns representing land primates when referring to other Black people. This was important, for they understood that these words will always be used against them if they kept using them. They understood that these words were meant not to help the race, but to keep them apart and divide them, so they could be easily brainwashed and turned against their fellow brothers and sisters. They also understood that they could never expect other races to stop negatively referring to them with such racist words if they kept it in their vocabularies. This, of course, did not stop racist people from using such words towards them, but Black people wholesale never used those words themselves again in their language to describe themselves or anyone else after this.

The Black people in America led the way, and all other Black cultures seemingly followed.

Black men earned their degrees at an astonishing rate. Schools that were offering degrees cheaply saw their admissions of Black people shoot up by a thousand percent and more. This was happening around the world. Black children took extra subjects in school to catch up with their schoolmates and counterparts. In many cases, they even surpassed them. In the many countries where education was free, Black people took advantage to stop no short of their Master's degree, or they went onwards and obtained their Doctorates. In places like America, where education was more expensive, Black people at first had to rely on cheaply offered degrees from "not for profit" schools who were reputable, with true education and learning in mind.

Black people learned to *properly* read trends, stocks, business profiles, and constitutional language and made it a part of their everyday education to invest time in learning what the laws of the land were, and who their *congressional and political representatives* were.

They learned and read. Those in prison learned and read. They learned new languages. They earned degrees. They kept reading and learning. A majority of the richer Black families and corporations donated resources and time to teach and invest in their fellow Black people, and money was directly given and used to push education as a primary focus.

This time, *for real.*

This had an astounding effect. More and more Black people were educating themselves correctly. More and more Black folks were learning and being taught a proper education. The increase in Black people with degrees began to shatter all expectations.

This was beginning to have an effect on the current system at the time. While many had now gained an education, there were not nearly as many jobs or work for them all. This was expected, but still frustrating. The Black Council wondered if it should recommend a limit to how much people should keep obtaining degrees, but decided against this. They knew it was expedient and important for the whole race to view education and learning as essential to their success, essential *to life itself.* It did not matter if there were no jobs, for this was the current state of affairs for them now anyway. It did not matter if institutions and corporations did not employ these newly minted Black degree holders. Many of these people without jobs were supported by the worldwide coordinated effort to play their part in furthering Black education.

There were some who, through life circumstance and cruel oppression or geographical location, was not given the opportunity to learn and gain knowledge the same way as others, but even for these people, they learned what they could, through reading and learning from books or verbal conversation with those who had gotten the opportunity to learn. The educational initiative could not be stopped. For them, the focus was not to obtain a degree, and obtain a high paying job, but to obtain knowledge. They would have the knowledge to know right from wrong. They would have the knowledge to know when political leaders were seeking to mislead and lie to them into voting against their best interests. They would have the knowledge to know when to vote and when to stand up for their rights. In places like America, it became the precedent of Black parents that no Black child must grow up without knowing the constitution and the bill of rights *by heart*. No Black child must get past the age of five, without knowing how to read at a beginner's level, and no Black individual, aged twelve and above should spend no less than four to five hours a day reading and studying and gaining new knowledge if they were in school and school age. This also applied to adults where it could. No matter what that knowledge was, where you worked, or your social and economic status.

A new trend was emerging. It became the new norm for Black people to learn and enjoy their education. More work needed to be done, and the process was slow. In fact, many years had passed. In other aspects of life, things were, for the most part, the same for Black people. Poverty persisted. Unjust, racist treatment still pervaded their society. Many learned, but many who were still left behind. Many children still grew up in homes, impoverished, and lacking in education and quality. Many people were still burdened by the comfortable, sleepy ignorance of abiding day by day in a system designed solely to keep them oppressed. Many were still living their lives, not knowing any better.

However, this was about to change. The Black council after many years decided that it was time to enact the next step of the plan, the next step towards progress. They would do away with all forms of distraction and waste. They would not only free their minds, but they would also free their bodies and souls. They would undertake the most massive efforts to stay away from any and all manners of vices and traps that would seek to destroy them, their minds, their goals, their objectives. They would resist temptation. They would resist distractions. They would refrain from violence. They would refrain from drugs. They would refrain from everything that harmed them.

They would rise above. They would *Elevate*.

* * * * *

The Elevating Movement

The media and news organizations were in a frenzy. All Black rappers had retired, and all Black singers refused to sing anything related to sex, violence, or drugs. There was no more rap being made. If hip hop songs were being produced, it was words and non-complicated rhyme used to push the importance of elevation of Black people, and rap language was only used to push the subject of love and inclusiveness. There were many Black figures and notable people already doing this, but now, more and more Black celebrities, actors, entertainers, and singers joined in. They all decided that they would no longer create or produce any media with themes of guns, violence, money, drugs, or sex.

Video ho's or video vixens as they were now being referred to, became an extinct job title in the Black race. Fewer and fewer Black women were seen shaking their butts, half-naked on television, Fewer Black girls were seen in porn or the adult entertainment industry. The Black women, who still aspired to show their beauty and talent, engaged in new Black-owned educational entertainment media, where they showcased and taught the arts and history. More and more Black people learned to play musical instruments. Black models still "modeled" and showcased their bodies to an extent, for this was an aspect of art too, but Black women and men as a whole declined any entertainment job that sought to exploit their bodies for sex or adult entertainment.

The entirety of Black people around the world engaged in this, and collectively embraced alternate forms of Black entertainment from other cultures, refraining from anything demoralizing or crude.

In America, BET was bought out and renamed from Black Entertainment Television *to Black Educational Television*. Programming changed. Gone were the days of the rap video, or the street gang, Black rap struggle, drug violence movie. Instead, this was replaced by men and women singing uplifting songs, and promoting arts-based media, whether religious or secular. There was enough media to be consumed that contained sex, drugs, and violence, and so Black people refrained from participating in this type of entertainment any further.

Drugs were banned. If anyone was found using drugs, it did not matter if it was a friend or family. That person was warned and then help was sought for them. If they refused to listen and kept up with doing drugs to the point of addiction, family and friends demanded they become admitted, even against their will, to drug treatment and detox centers. Drugs were not to be sold or used by Black people anymore, unless needed for strictly medicinal purposes. The effort to push and legalize marijuana was also abandoned. This made a lot of Black people upset at first, but Black people realized that their minds must be clear and that any forms of drugs, whether addicting or not, must be shunned unless medically expedient or necessary.

No more Crack, Cocaine, or Heroin was *produced, sold, used, or distributed* by Black people. The overall numbers of drug-related incidences and deaths began to decrease in Black communities worldwide. The numbers of young Black people dying of drugs and overdose fell so sharply, that many wondered if the statistical data was off or skewed. Black people began to be careful of anyone using drugs and began to shun all forms of it in the streets and their places of abode.

Drinking and Smoking were also heavily decreased. If there were people who still insisted on drinking and consuming alcohol, it was limited to one drink a week and decreased to the point where it was only consumed on the occasional social outing, or heavily neutered to the point, where they were essentially drinking diluted water. Heavy smokers sought help to quit, and it was not easy, but with determination, they did.

Black people began to refrain from going to clubs. If you wanted to dance, you danced at home.

If you wanted to meet people, you did so through the three avenues as guided by the *Black Council*: Church, School, or Work. There were little to no Black people seen partying out late at night. Black people would instead, stay home, and study into the late hours of the night. Instead of dancing to the latest pop song at the club, they video conferenced each other and danced to the song at home. Black women refrained from seeking out the next club to hop to, and instead, spent time at home, either learning or teaching their children or families something new.

Black people began to stop all of their *promiscuous* endeavors. There were fewer and fewer Black children who did not know who their father was. Black men and women sought to keep one partner, and when things didn't work out for whatever reason, they spent more time on themselves, their children and their families, instead of immediately finding the next woman or man to date.

This took many years to accomplish as well, but the overall family size of Black families decreased. People were still having large families if they wanted, but they must first satisfy self-imposed key criteria, such as having a terminal degree, and possess a well-paying job, to properly feed and take care of their children. Also, more and more Black men and women chose to get married and stay married for over a year, before deciding to have children.

Those who were young and dated, refrained from unsafe sexual practices, and if they decided that they wanted to engage in sexual activity, they always used proper protection to prevent accidental pregnancies and STD transmissions.

In addition to everything Black people were doing collectively around the world, efforts were now made to decrease the overall illegal gun ownership of the Black race. In America, guns continued to be bought and sold by Black people, but not without a license and proper documentation. Black people overall, refused to carry guns and simply stopped using them in self-defense altercations. *Violence on a whole* was looked down upon. All forms of violence was abandoned and shunned. If there was a need to protest, peaceful sit-ins, and boycotts were organized.

Black people no longer participated in riots. When in the course of protesting, the protests were not marked by any shouting or corralling. Instead, Black people would sing. They would sing of their struggle, and the need for the change they were seeking to protest for. Weapons were no longer carried in the streets as tools to harm. They were kept only as a method of self-defense, and to defend their lives and their homes. Black people stopped shooting and killing each other. They stopped being responsible for murders or manslaughter. The number of stabbings and killings performed by members of the Black race decreased. Street gangs began to become rarer and scarcer.

They began to clean up their communities. Graffiti was only used as an art expression through commissioned murals and carefully chosen places. All other graffiti was unanimously agreed upon to be either cleaned up, erased, or disposed of where feasible.

Black people stopped cursing. They stopped disrespecting other people and also stopped letting "street cred" be the primary driver of respect. Instead "educational cred" was the new form of street currency.

Many Black criminals vowed to stop breaking the law. Laziness was also thus abandoned. Many found honest work in cleaning up the society, and self-policing. Black communities began to look pristine. There were no young Black men seen loitering in the streets, no young Black men "hanging out" doing nothing, looking for trouble.

Black people began to take more pride in their homes and where they lived. Not a speck of garbage could be seen. Everyone desired clean environments and all worked towards making it so. When such people who wanted to destroy the cleanliness of those who worked hard to clean up their environment would thrust garbage and litter in their community spitefully in the dark of the night, the whole neighborhood would come out and help clean it up.

Black people all over now cherished deeper respect for their community and the environment and sought ways and means to keep their homes and communities free of clutter, garbage, and trash.

Black people stopped buying expensive brand name sneakers. Sales of brand name sneakers plummeted. Young black men, as a whole, also immediately stopped *fighting* over sneakers. Black people began to put their extra money towards their education first, then after, they spent their money on buying regular, just as usable, no-name branded goods and products. The excess money not spent on these wasteful enterprises was saved or donated to other Black people suffering in other parts of the country or world. Black women stopped going to their hairdressers to get their hair done and stopped using chemicals of all forms in their hair, no longer destroying, abusing, or foolishly coloring it to unnatural colors. Beauty products were used to look decent and presentable, but excess hair and makeup were avoided.

The Black diet began to change. Gone, was the excess consumption of fried foods. Black people still ate these things, but now in greatly decreased moderation. The use of sugar and salt was also greatly decreased. Instead, the use of vegetables and beneficial foods were increased. For those who owned land, a greater focus was placed on developing Black-owned farms and eating more organically. Pork was also greatly decreased from the diet, and many sought out vegetarian lifestyles and principles to incorporate it into their diets.

Obese Black people, around the world, began to exercise. They exercised like there was fire beneath them. As a result of this, the new incidences of diabetes and strokes and heart attacks greatly decreased for the Black population as a whole, and more and more Black people with these chronic conditions began to live longer healthier lives. *That is when they weren't being murdered whilst performing their exercise, or going about their daily lives.*

Wholesale tolerance and respect for all, began to be a primary driver in everyday life. No more disrespect for other cultures or races. No more racial or lifestyle slurs were seen amongst Black people. All Black citizens, regardless of lifestyle choice, sexual or gender-wise, was accepted. *No more hate by the Black community was shown to Black transgender people.* No more mistreatment of people who identified as homosexual or alternate sexual identification. For those who were of religious faith, they became even more religious. Many endeavored to attend religious services once a week, and for those who did not believe in religion, they still upheld a great moral standard, that permeated their lives and their relationships.

Prisoners who had thus served their time and were released from prison, refrained from any activity that would place them in direct association or connection with their prior crimes. The recidivism rate declined considerably. Those who had spent time in prison, and were thus released, had earned their degrees and began to immediately work towards improving their community through any means available to them.

Black people began to do many other things that began to improve their lives, the lives of others, and the overall world. They were as we say, "cleaning themselves up". They were lacing up their proverbial "bootstraps". Many achieved successes. Many succeeded in uplifting their families, their lives, and their communities the world over.

The *Black Council* was overjoyed with their success. From the beginning of the endeavor to now, it had been many years. Some of the older members of the council had passed away, and new members had taken their place, yet they carried on the initial objective, well into the future. All Black people in the world were joined and engaged in the conscious effort to improve their wellbeing and to focus on making life better for themselves, as well as for others along the way. All that was left now, was to enact the final step in the plan.

They would seek to change the ways the system was still seeking to depress them. They would take the bold step to come forward to the light and show themselves to the world. They would wrest the one thing that was keeping them back from complete success, from completing their overall mission.

They would gain *Political Power.*

* * * * *

Political Power

It started small at first. More and more Black political representatives were gaining steam and becoming elected. Many smaller congressional seats that now, no one paid much attention to, and that no one felt would make a difference. These initial smaller seats were quickly snatched up. Next, came time to obtain higher positional seats. This part would not be so easy to reproduce, for many a representative, many a cardinal, many a parliamentarian seat was won through less than *objectively idealistic* means. Many Black political representatives had to agree with the agenda of other misaligned colleagues, in order to get elected and to attain power. But once in power, the elected representatives quickly went back to expounding their core beliefs in representing what was morally right. At first, this was as with all the other previous steps, slow and cautious, however, advances were made.

After the first *true* Black president was elected, the doors flung open. Senate seats were won. Key districts were now under the governance of a Black representative. Parliaments and Judiciaries saw an influx of Black modulation, all wielding increased power than what was *previously* allowed or given them before.

Prior to this last step, the world observed, watching Black people enact the steps in their plan to elevate the race, and many applauded the genuine efforts of the Black race to achieve their goals. Many cheered on, as many Black people turned away from their vices and violence. Many were impressed with the kindness and mercy shown, exemplified, and exhibited by all Black people the world over, despite the terrible injustices and unfair treatment they still faced. They watched as they joined and included other races, and worked together to promote harmony and defeat hatred and bigotry, not only for themselves but for all other races who suffered against these tragedies. Many respected the earnest determination and patience shown and hoped for the success of the movement and the success of the plan. Many supported, and many hoped.

But *some* feared.

They were afraid, for they believed that if this movement, this undertaking, was left unchecked, these so-called *"African Blacks"* would attempt to take over the world. Many condescendingly thought that the *African Blacks* had played a good game, but it was now time to be happy with what they had and to pat themselves on the back at a job well done.

After all, didn't they now have equal status with the rest of better off races? I mean, **true** equal status? Did they not manage to eliminate violence and drugs within their communities? Were they not now well respected? They had all collectively increased their education and knowledge. Did they not achieve something grand and special?

It is important to remember that this small group of people, these opposing forces, were **not** made up of just one group of people, or one definitive race. This was not as simple as White people against Black people. Neither was it Europeans against Muslims. Sadly, many interspersing sects of people of many races and cultures decided that this wasn't *good or acceptable* for their racist beliefs, and the most heartbreaking thing above it all was not that these people were racist, no. The worst aspect was that many of them were of the Black race as well.

Before this final step, these forces were not as offended, nor were they as troubled. It was, for a time, amusing for some of them. As such, they sat back and let the *Black Council* direct and dictate their plan. They let Black people enjoy their successes and watched on as they began to elevate themselves as a whole and show that they could be a force for good and achieve their goals.

But now, they were offended. The *African Blacks* had managed to do something that deeply disrespected them, for they sought to reverse systematic depression once and for all. They sought to change statutes and laws to help get rid of injustices, put in place by a system to keep them down, emasculate them, unfairly punish them and keep them poor and downtrodden.

For you see, they had achieved political power.

This power was indeed significant. This was now *real* power. Just as the corporations and select people in power in our present time now yield. Power to change and enact laws to benefit themselves, just as the forces opposing them had done for so long. This was true power. They would now keep pushing the envelope until more and more laws and statutes were changed to benefit the minorities. The *Black Council* had achieved the ultimate victory. This was the true end of the plan. They would use their power benevolently and continue to elevate the race and help other races as well. They would continue to do good. They would not be tempted to be corrupt despite those who would see the race fail once more. They would study history and learn lessons from the past, and they would never abuse their power, as those in power do now.

They would only change laws to do away with unfair and unjust precedents, and truly free their fellow downtrodden people from systematic oppression and then seek to live this life as all others, and enjoy some modicum of decency in life, on this one planet we all share.

Black people the world over had now felt as if they had found their true place. Injustice and inequality amongst all races still existed, but they had found the formula to elevating the race, and it was working splendidly. Black people were raising their kids in comfort and happiness. The hope and potential of the race was no longer being limited, and the world seemingly began to get just a little bit better.

However, as rosy as this picture was made to look, the powers that feared a fictitious Black takeover would not *allow* such things to persist.

They were now moving their shadowy hands in the background, working to thwart the progress of the race, as they had once done. The happiness seemingly gained by the Black race over many years was not to last, for the *Black Separation* was coming.

The Speech of Animals

"What words in rhyme can reach the height of its peak?
For Animals now talk, Yes, now they can Speak."

God came down one day and visited the Earth. He saw the state of affairs of all humans. He watched the cruelty and suffering of animals at the hands of some people. He watched how some people cared little for the animals he placed in man's care. He had done this many times before, but he observed it all once again. He considered how they felt. He watched how they longed to be treated. He watched how they lived their lives. He read their thoughts. He pondered it.

He then declared that *all animals shall now be able to speak and use human language to communicate with humans.*

Then he left.

* * * * *

Francine was home playing with her cat, Tuna, when Tuna suddenly stopped, and asked Francine for some water.

Francine was a kind soul and loving master for Tuna, and she loved her very much. Tuna was the daughter of a female cat owned by a woman down the street. This cat was the "mistress" for all the other male cats on the block. Everyone knew this and accepted it.

She was, for all intents and purposes, a ho. Francine would often playfully joke with Tuna and tell her that her "momma is a ho".

Tuna's mother had brought her kitten to the step of Francine's house and left her there. Can you imagine, a cat knowing she wanted to abandon her kitten? I suppose we should just be glad she didn't eat her.

The woman who owned Tuna's mother had seen that she had brought her kitten to Francine's house and told Francine she could keep the kitten if she wanted.

So, Francine kept her.

Francine raised her, and Tuna grew up fat and comfortable. She was well taken care of and loved Francine.

Francine, in her joyful playing with Tuna, didn't at first realize what just happened. Tuna was thirsty and just asked her for some water, so she turned right away and went to the kitchen to grab her the water bowl.

As she was at the sink, filling the water bowl, she suddenly stopped. She dropped the bowl on the floor and ran back to the living room.

Tuna? Francine asked. Did you just ask for water?

Tuna looked at her, with somewhat of a shocked cat expression on her face, and answered.

"Yes, Mommy. I'm thirsty"

Francine screamed. How? What! Tuna, you can talk? Am I going crazy? Oh God!

Tuna, at the sight of seeing Francine screaming, started to scream too. It was so weird, that when Francine heard Tuna scream out, she stopped screaming.

How are you able to talk Tuna? How is this possible?

"I don't know Mommy! I always wanted to talk to you and tell you how much I loved you, but you seemed to not ever understand me. But now you can finally understand! I hear myself talking to you, and you are understanding me. I don't know how, but we can do it!"

How? Francine asked. Still very much surprised.

"I don't know mommy, but now that you can understand me, and I can talk to you, I wanted to ask you, why do you always make a weird "meow" sound to me whenever I talk to you? What does "meow" mean? And why do you always refer to yourself as a ho? What is a "ho" mommy?"

* * * * *

"Breaking News! Animals start talking and conversing in human language!" The news headlines and social media reports were everywhere, it was broadcasting all around the world.

As millions of Dogs and cats and sundry house pets began to converse with their owners, thousands of people started posting videos to the internet and many streaming sites, of conversations they had with their animals. One person posted a full conversation his Dog even had with another Dog as he was walking him near the park down the street.

Their conversation was actually very contemptuous, petty, and vulgar.

"Hey you, hey you, you stink, let me smell your ass"

"Yeah, you stink too buddy. You can smell mines as long as you let me smell yours."

"What did you eat today?"

My master served me chunks of meat my friend. What about you?"

"Ah, I got dry food today."

"Aha-haa your master is a cheap bastard. My master gives me everything."

"Well, at least I got to smell that new bitch that moved in last week. She smelt like grass and perfume."

"Oh, you did? Damn. She was kinda hot. I wanna mount that b…"

The guy cut his video there. Their conversation had become too explicit.

As the days went by, more and more people were embracing it faster than what was originally thought. Animals were conversing with all humans, and of course, amongst themselves. Many were shocked to know that humans could now understand their conversation, and many surprisingly took to show their displeasure with the human race. The poor zookeepers and animal caretakers got the worst of it. Some of the animals were downright abusive and cantankerous. They laughed at the zookeepers for having to clean up their waste and joked how humans thought they were the most intelligent, but they, the animals, have been pretending to not know how to clean up their feces for ages now, and how they always take joy watching the humans do it. Small arrogant cats, they said, were the only ones who didn't hide that they knew how to clean up after themselves.

Monkeys especially would die laughing when pieces of feces they flung, landed on people. They said we deserved it for saying that we came from them. In the course of such rantings and mirth amongst themselves, one monkey would shout *"Evolution!"* and they would all burst out laughing. They were highly amused at how wrong the humans were. They said if Man could not see how blatant it was that a higher power had created them, they wouldn't say a thing. They would just laugh at the humans and their blatant stupidity.

The monkeys seemed to enjoy making fun of humans for some reason.

As the world adjusted to the new norm, the world was alight with noise. Humans could not sleep, for there was no longer such things as creature sounds or nighttime sounds of the forest that humans have been accustomed to go to sleep to. Instead, it was nonstop chatter from the crickets, birds, and sundry species alike, who remained awake at night.

"So, anybody wanna have sex?"

"Yeah me, me! I'm ready and able."

"Ok you got it; I'm heading your way now"

No one could ever understand why, and it was a curious thing, that some of the nighttime animals appeared obsessed with copulating. Curious indeed.

Many of the smaller birds wisely gathered materials for their nests at night, when the humans were asleep. Said they: *"It's just safer. We try to avoid getting run over during the day."* The pigeons and the skewers were generally in disagreement with this, as they heavily relied on food from the humans during the day, and slept in buildings at night.

"Did you stock enough food for Winter?" One pregnant squirrel asked her spouse.

"Yeah, I did, but you do realize it's still early Spring. You haven't even given birth yet."

"So? Just get back to work. We gotta stock up for the Winter."

The female animals were, not to anyone's surprise, very bossy.

Many people complained that these conversations went on all night and that it often disturbed the humans so much, that some even shouted at them through their windows to shut up. It became a whole worldwide thing. Humans couldn't get enough sleep because the animals stayed up all night looking for sex. Many of the animals apologized, as they felt ashamed of their promiscuous endeavors, but some refused to thus entertain any such pontifications. They were not ashamed at all. They would curse back at the humans, and blame them, saying that it was all their fault and that humans shouldn't complain, because we make a lot of noise during the day and disturb them too.

With particular animosity, the Crickets, when they were shouted on by humans, would tell the humans to kiss their ass, and screamed even louder over the din, asking for sex from whoever was nearby.

* * * * *

Tuna began licking herself. She repeated her questions to Francine, asking about the "meowing" sound Francine would make to her whenever she spoke. Francine said that she never meowed to Tuna at all. She said she always spoke to her, but Tuna always "meowed" back to her.

"Isn't that your language Tuna?" Francine asked.

"No Mommy, I always spoke to you just like how we are talking now. You always "meow-ed" back to me."

"Very Interesting," Francine said. "So we hear a specific sound from animals, and animals hear the same sound in response from us when we talk back to them?"

"I think you are right mommy. Now mommy, what is a "ho"?

Francine said that Tuna shouldn't worry about it.

Tuna continued talking.

"Mommy, I'm thirsty, can I have some water now?"

Francine went and got the bowl from where she dropped it and brought some water for Tuna.

"Tuna, just tell me one thing, why do you think this is happening?"

"I don't know Mommy," Tuna said, between lapping up water with her little tongue, *"But aren't you glad we can talk to each other properly now?"*

"I am, Tuna, but doesn't it feel weird to you?"

"Not really. I've always talked to you anyway, it just seemed like you couldn't understand me, but now you can. Is this a bad thing Mommy?"

"No, but it just feels very weird to me. I guess I'm just used to hearing you "meow" and that's it. I was just a little scared and surprised that my baby cat can talk to me now."

"Have you never been able to talk to the other animals before?" Tuna inquired.

"No, of course not Tuna, Humans and animals are different species. We can live together, but we were never able to talk to each other in Human language before."

Francine then went on to explain about different animals and species, and how each animal had a different sound, and a different way to communicate with humans. Tuna listened. Then she continued.

"Well, we were always able to talk to each other."

"Really?" Francine asked. This was another revolutionary discovery to Francine, nay, to humans altogether.

"So cats can talk to Dogs and understand them? Rabbits can talk to foxes?"

"Yes Mommy, we can understand each other clearly. I talk to other animals all the time. To me, their words come across as clear as you and me talking right now, so I never realized that other animals spoke differently."

"Wow Tuna! We didn't know that. So wait, that rat you killed the other day. It was screaming as you held it by the tail. It was talking to you?"

"Yes, Mommy."

"Wait, then what did it say?"

"It was begging me for its life, but at the same time angry at me and threatened that his father would gnaw my ears off when I slept. When you saw the rat and jumped on the bed, I was telling you not to be scared, because I was gonna kill it and protect you."

"Oh. So the rat was begging for its life?"

"Yes, Mommy."

"But you killed it anyway?"

Yes, Mommy, I didn't want it to hurt you. It was cursing at you and saying that you don't leave enough food out for them. So they have to scavenge for scraps, and that it wasn't his fault. I got mad and crushed his neck. He deserved it."

"Wait Tuna, maybe you shouldn't do that anymore."

"Why Mommy? I always kill rats when I see them. They don't like you or respect you. So when I see them, I kill them."

"So...what about when Dogs chase cats...?

"We have had our differences. Many Dogs feel they should live alone with Humans, and we small cats should go live like our larger related family members. We say the same thing to them. We constantly disagree sometimes, so we fight about it. But most times, we get along peacefully. Especially when we both have the interest of our families at heart."

"Wow, ok Tuna, I didn't know you knew or realized all of this."

"I do Mommy. I remember from the moment I opened my eyes and saw you. I remember something carrying me around, then it put me down on the ground and it was so cold! Then I remember you picking me up. I remember your smell and I remember when I opened my eyes and saw you for the first time smiling at me."

"Oh Tuna! That's so sweet!" So you remember everything from a baby?"

"Yes, Mommy."

"Ok. That is very interesting. I don't think people realize that animals can remember everything from a baby onwards."

"Most of us can. Tuna replied. "Some choose to forget. Many Dogs say they choose not to remember. They say the memory of them taken from their brothers and sisters is just too painful and so they choose to remember meeting their human family for the first time instead."

"Oh, I see," Francine replied.

* * * * *

The pronunciation came in the middle of the day. The animals had gathered in all areas of their home continents and had decided it was time to congregate and discuss what was going on. Large numbers of animals could be seen in varying parts of their habitats. Animal representatives from all species were in attendance. It was decided that the birds, due to their mobility, would be the messengers to spread the information worldwide on what was happening.

Each species and animal representative addressing the issues they had amongst them. At the end of such meetings, birds would fly everywhere and spread the news and information as necessary.

After all these gatherings, it was decided that animals should thus have a say in the matters of the world. This, they concluded, was for the better of all. They would elect a specific representative, who was then to go and speak to mankind.

But who should be the representative? Who should go speak on behalf of all animals? A vote was cast by all animals worldwide. Dogs made the compelling case that they were already close to humans, thus it would be easy to talk to them. Some species of birds like the Parrot and the Macaw decided that it should fall to their kind, as they could essentially talk already, and the humans were amused with them, as they could use their voices to mimic human language, so it would be easy to communicate with the humans. The larger animals like the Elephant and Hippo made the argument that they had an imposing presence, and thus the humans would respect what they had to say. The larger cats like the Jaguar and the Leopard stayed quiet. They were simply not interested in being a representative to anyone, much less to the humans. After long deliberations, it was wisely decided that the already domesticated animals should lead the front, as they were already accustomed to the human ways. As such, the Dog was chosen as chief animal representative.

While many agreed on this, many species voiced their pejorative dissent to this plan, and some to a greater degree showed outright disgust.

Of such were the Crocodile, and to no one's surprise, The Snake.

Said the Snake:

"We do not trussst the Humans'sss for they hate us'sss with a passsssion. We will not agree to these'sss terms'sss to

have the Dog sssspeak for us'sss nor will we ssseek alliances'sss with the realms'sss of men."

The Crocodile, a little more amenable to the effort, but still against the whole thing, only expressed dismay at how the Humans would treat them. Said the Croc:

"We do not have a quarrel with the humans. But they do not like us and how we live. They will sooner save the zebra and the wildebeest, of which we need to eat, than to make concessions for us. We can subsist on dead carrion like the Vulture, but we also seek raw, living flesh as sustenance. In addition to this, they see us as ugly and dirty. Many of our kind, through fear and self-defense, has killed the Human. Will they trust us after all this?"

At these words, many of the other wild animals agreed. They and their species had killed many a human. Surely this could not be forgiven. They did not want to now be treated worse than what they had already endured by human hand.

But the Great Gorilla spoke up. He didn't talk much, but when he stood up to speak, all animals listened.

"I do not think we should be afraid of seeking to speak to the human, for this cannot make our lives any worse than

it already is. Some of us live in captivity, never to be free. Many of us are slaughtered, whether for food or fun. Some of us indeed, hate how the human has treated us. But we cannot sit back, now that they can understand us, and not do something thus. We should seek to now repair the divide; we should now seek to use this opportunity to forge an understanding between the human and us. To your declarations of distrust, I present to you this argument: How many of us thus eat each other for survival? Are we that much different than the human? To those who eat the grass of the field, you do the least harm; for you do not eat other animal-kind, and to this, you are the most commendable. But to those who do, you do it not through hate, but through the need to survive. For you must by all means survive. The humans have taken much, and sometimes committed grave sins to the animal order. This is why the Tasmanian Tiger and the Black Rhino is no longer with us. As such, we must now take steps to forge a good understanding between man and beast, for this opportunity was given to us by He who created us. We must not, like the human, waste what we are given."

Upon hearing these strong, wise words, all the animals agreed. The Crocodile species and their cousins resigned to see how the humans would handle their case, for they would not be resolved to eat grass, but would subsist on carrion for the time being. But the Snake, in defiance, voiced his further disdain for the humans and stated that no matter what, they would never come to an understanding. They said they would sooner leave and find somewhere to live far away, perhaps deep underground, where they could be left alone. They slithered away, muttering that all animals should thus go back to how they were, and if they continued in this way, they would surely come to regret their decision. The other animals watched on, as they slinked away into the darkness, never to be seen again.

* * * * *

"Tuna, Can I ask you something? How do you see us? How do you see the world? Do you think what humans do is good?"

"I don't understand Mommy" Tuna replied.

"Well, I mean, about having animals in zoos and stuff. Do you think we should let all the animals go?"

"Oh, I see what you mean. No, I think most of them are happy."

"Really?"

"*Yes, Mommy. Generally speaking, I don't think the animals in the zoos and other places mind. They are happy to interact with you. Well, most of them are. Some are angry and do constantly say that they would kill you if they got the chance. I think humans are wonderful, because you hear them say that, but you still take care of them.*"

"Well Tuna, we never knew they were saying that."

"*Oh yes, that's right. I forgot, Mommy. As I understand it, most of us animals really like humans, and want to live peacefully with you, and want to be taken care of. Just like how you take care of me, but many sadly don't get the chance.*"

"I know Tuna, I feel sorry for the animals in the zoos."

"*No, Mommy, not the zoos. Those animals are ok. They usually feel well taken care of, and eat well. Even the more hateful ones say they enjoy a luxurious lifestyle. They just don't like humans for some reason.*"

"So what do you mean Tuna?" Francine asked.

"*I meant the animals that humans mistreat. I see those animal commercials come on the TV all the time. I see how my fellow family members are treated.*"

"Oh no Tuna, you would see those commercials?"

"Yes, Mommy. I would watch as my fellow animals would be suffering in those cages. I have heard stories of animals being beaten and abused. I even heard strange tales of humans making us fight one another for sport or entertainment. I always hoped this wasn't true. Is it true Mommy?"

"It's true Tuna. Those are some of the bad things that people have done to animals."

"Oh. Thank you for telling me the truth Mommy."

"Tuna, do you get upset when you see stuff like that?"

"Yes, very much. When I see my fellow brothers and sisters in those tiny cages, all scared and begging for someone to help them, I thank God that I have you. You will never leave me like that, right Mommy?"

"Never, Tuna. I would never let something like that happen to you."

Tuna jumped into Francine's lap and sat down to go to sleep.

"Thank you, Mommy. I love you. Please know that I will do anything for you. I wish I could help my brothers and

sisters out there, but I know that I don't want to ever do anything to make you or any other human upset with me. Please help them, mommy. Ok?"

"I wish I could, Tuna, but I ca…"

Tuna looked up. *"You can't help them, mommy?"*

Francine thought about it before she answered.

"You know what? Yes, I can help them. I can help them Tuna. I promise you; I will help as much of them as I can, ok? Now you can go ahead and get some sleep. When you wake up, we can talk some more."

"Ok Mommy, Thank you."

Tuna drifted off to sleep. Francine watched her as she slept. She purred quietly as she slept, safely in her lap. Not worrying about a thing.

Francine turned on the TV and went to the news. She watched as animals being filmed in all parts of the world were crying out for help, and she cried silently for a little, for she could now understand exactly what they were saying.

She then took the remote, and turned off the TV, and got up, with Tuna, still sleeping, held in her arms, and bent down and unplugged the set.

The Speech of Animals II

*'Tis' the second tale, of the Animal's speech in
Conjecture, A Lesson in Wisdom, for The Dog will now
Lecture."*

My fellow human brothers and sisters, we have been
friends with you from time immemorial. Many,
many centuries span, in which we have had
friendship with all humans, and deep friendships indeed, for
we love your kind. For those of us domesticated and adapted
to human life, we wish to always be friends and deeper yet,
family members in your nuclear unit. But now, I bring tidings
of all animal species. As man and beast can now, with a clear
mind and depth, understand each other. It has been decided
that my species, the Dog, would stand as representative to you
all, seeking to disseminate the matters of the animal kingdom,
and what must be thus outlined. It is of our consensus, that

animal-kind must have a say in all matters of the planet, of which we all share."

The Dog stood proudly at the pulpit of the United Nations floor assembly. He was a Collie-Shepherd mix, wise and smart, but also very attractive. He was accompanied by the Doberman and the Poodle as they stood next to him, along with a small regiment of seven birds, one as a messenger to each continent, who would relay the information as received once the assembly was concluded.

The meeting came to be, after the Dog made the public announcement that animals sought an audience with the humans at the general assembly. For a time, it was debated between nations if this should be allowed. However, a little frightened at the thought of backlash at denying such a request, the UN security council convened and voted to allow the animal his day. They would be allowed to speak at the general assembly. An assembly was convened specifically for the animal, for humans were eager and frankly curious to hear what animals had to say.

The Dog continued.

"We do not present ourselves today in a manner to show any speculation of threat, but of compromise. We, the animal

species seek an understanding with all mankind. We know that this planet is ruled by your hand, whether for good or worse, and we do not seek to impose a rebellion, or thus incite any violence towards man. It is solely my gumption to speak for the animal kingdom, and present our "recommendations" for a happy and peaceful life, between human and beast."

The Dog paused for effect, and stooped down and took a few laps of water from his bowl under the podium to let his words sink in. After a few moments, he spoke again.

"We want to first ask for leniency, as we endeavor to collectively apologize for the lives lost in previous encounters between man and animal. We want to extend our sad condolences to families of all humans, who sadly lost a loved one by animal attack or defense. Surely, almost the entirety of the animal species can assure you, even this very day, that it was done only out of fear and instinct to survive. Of the most egregious of us, down to the most docile, this fact is true. We with deep regret and olive branch in hand, apologize to all humans."

These words seemed to strike a chord in the audience and many nodded in approval. However, those same words, spoken out of a desire to appease, only served to annoy.

"What, so you mean to tell us, that you want to now apologize for animals killing humans?"

Others spoke out: "Then you *always* knew what you were doing."

It caused a slight commotion among the members of the representative countries. After all, it was now understood that when an animal killed a human, they *knew* what they were doing. Humans would put an animal down for biting or harming another human, but it was always believed that the *dumb* animal did not know better. But how should they respond now, when it is now made known, that the actions animals took to thus slay the human, were quite frankly, deliberate. The birds, ready to fly away should it get amorous, opened their wings, to take off.

The Dog listened for a while and then spoke up.

"My beloved friends, you must not be so harsh, nor should you be so unforgiving. Surely, you cannot count the sheer number of animals who happily lay down their lives, whether knowingly or unknowingly as food, protection, and sustenance for all humans. Many of our species are thus bred for little more than livestock. We have all, as part of the animal kingdom, accepted this order. We do not stand here to demand

rightful apologies for these sentiments, or the cruel admonishing of humans to our kind for centuries, for we clearly understand the precedents of the natural order. You are the top predator of the planet. We must abide by this. But animals are also thus killed for sport and entertainment, by the not so good among you, of which we carry deep-seated wounds and pain in our hearts. Do you not think animals share a family structure? Do you not feel we have kindred spirit and friends amongst ourselves? Or that we lack memory of the past? Surely, if we can offer the olive branch in regards to this, then you, my dear esteemed masters and friends, can at least try to acknowledge and accept our amicable sentiments, as we attempt to reach a mutual understanding. I ask you thus, let me continue."

After listening to these words, many of the audience agreed to settle down. Simply put, the Dog's words were completely fair and true.

The Dog continued.

"As we work towards an agreement, we wanted to ask that the animal species be thus represented in human councils and in higher facets of government. We feel we can provide a never before seen light to the decisions of man, as we all continue to live on this planet. We do not know the purpose we were given speech to speak plainly to you, but we want to

take every opportunity to not waste this gift that all animal life has now been given. We seek only to have an animal as a "friend" and advisor to every president in every country."

The audience gasped. The Dog had asked for power to be given to animals beyond what the humans had ever seriously pre-empted to give. An animal standing next to every president of every country? To help advise? What sort of madness was this? Should the animal be the Vice-Animal President of America? Or the Deputy Prime Beast Minister of Agriculture in New Zealand? This appeared absurd.

The Dog, receptive to what the assembly was thinking, continued his speech.

"It is not, for the sake of power we request this adjustment, but for the good of all. Further, we do not seek power as such that we would hold a human originated position, but only to serve as an advisor to the President and leader of each respective country. We would seek only to advise and guide in matters of animal relatedness and the planet, and never will we insert any logic into matters pertaining to man only. As an example, we would ask the President of the United States to choose, of his volition, an animal representative, who may thus serve as a guide to animal

matters, and serve as one of his many personal advisors. Of a truth, this is sort of what happens already. Do not your Presidents have some sort of house companion? Does not the Queen of England make friend with my English cousin, the Corgi? We seek to change nothing, but to simply add to the relationship.

After a short pause, many seemed to agree with this, and shouted "Fair!" into their prompters, at this suggestion. Many, however, whispered to themselves quietly.

As the speech continued, many people wondered how the animals were so intelligent. How could it be that they were unable to speak to us all this time? Surely, they could have found a way to communicate these sentiments to the human race prior?

Now, the time had come, for the Dog had one final request before wrapping up his speech. This would be the ultimate invocation; the prime request. For in this request, lay the future hope of many of the remaining species in the animal kingdom, but at the same time, the biggest risk of failure. This request was just that important; for they would seek to ask the humans to do something they did not like, something they would have little desire to do, something they would surely deny the animal kingdom, for it would cost them the precious money and amenities they so cared about and valued.

The animals would have the humans cease to destroy any further, the animal habitat, and by extension, the environment.

* * * * *

At the prior meetings, when the animals had earlier convened, several cases were discussed as of prime importance. One of them was the outright stoppage of killing animals for food. This was agreed upon as essential to survival to some species, but it was ultimately shot down as unreasonable, for they well knew that the humans would sooner rebel against this and kill animals in greater numbers should the animal kingdom seek to implore this request. Essentially, they knew the humans would not agree to this request, not due to retaliatory or ornery function, but instead, for sheer fear of starvation. The animals realized it would be foolish to ask humans to stop eating the fowl of the air, or the beast of the field, or the fish of the sea. This was something, all animals knew, that they must continue to endure, until the end of time.

The next part of the agenda was then, to request access to higher government to help provide guidance by the animal, in planetary matters. It was agreed upon by all, that this could very well be beneficial to animal and man alike, for now, they would now be able to have a voice, however small, at the highest levels of human power. Thus with hope, they would attempt to sway their elected leaders from such abuses of life and planet, such as war or continued nuclear weapons testing and uranium enrichment.

It was agreed upon, that as mentioned by the Dog in the upcoming assembly, that animals were never to interfere with matters pertaining to man, such as inter-racial matters, for this was human upon human violence, and had nothing to do with the animals. They were also never to influence how humans should spend their money concerning personal wealth. A watch was to be placed on each appointed animal, and if such animals were to turn and begin to do this, they would be "dealt" with by other animals. Animals could see, smell and hear hundreds of times better than the humans, so they would easily know if an animal was doing this, and seldom could they hide, even behind closed door, or shielded room.

The final request, or prime request was the problematic one. They knew that it would almost appear presumptuous for the animal to ask the human to stop such activities that destroy, and not to further harm or disrupt the animal's home, or its habitat. They would be walking a fine line in suggesting such a thing as this, for man did as they pleased, and would simply become angry at the thought of the animals telling them they must stop the harmful destruction of the planet, the harmful destruction of the animal abode and the harmful destruction of the environment. They knew this was dangerous indeed, but as the Great Gorilla pointed out, they must not waste this great opportunity.

It was decided that the Dog would speak as eloquently as he could, and seek to broker a common understanding first, then when the human began to empathetically agree with them, they would incite the prime request.

The Dog, after a few days, prepared his speech, and with the blessing of the whole animal kingdom, all fish, bird and mammal species, along with mostly all reptiles, except the dubious snake, of course, he made the request known that the animal kingdom sought an audience with mankind.

* * * * *

Before continuing his speech, the Dog requested another bowl of water, for his first bowl was done, and his throat was dry. He was very nervous. As soon as the water arrived, he took a few laps then cleared his throat. As he cleared his throat for the final passage of his speech, he stopped and looked around at the assembly. Here was the moment of truth; this was the time. The animal kingdom was all in agreement; *man must stop the abuse of the planet.* There were many reasons for this, one being solely to protect and preserve the already massively decreased numbers of their fellow animals. Another would be due to the poisoning of many animal's natural habitats. Many imperative reasons enveloped the foundations of the prime request, but still yet the Dog, knowing the most likely reaction of the humans, hesitated to begin.

Many humans did not yet realize this, but this is and always was, the sole reason behind the drive of many animals to unceasingly copulate. They were defenseless to Man in how he conducted his affairs on the planet. Many species were on the brink of being wiped out. Animals knew they must do something to preserve their numbers, and as such, animals began having sex. Lots of sex. Some fish species and mammals were huge proponents of this. Even the Dog, in times past, used to have a litter with but one pup, but after seeing their numbers diminish in the old world, they began to produce larger litters to counteract this. Now, mostly all animals do this to an extent, with some larger animals still preferring to produce one offspring at a time, but this is not the norm for the animal kingdom anymore.

Many animals echo these reproductive machinations. Said the Pig: *"We will birth several piglets at a time, for the humans eat us at an astonishingly rapid rate."* Many animals, like the rabbit, also hold this sentiment, and thus copulate, like well, Rabbits.

The Dog was still hesitant to speak. He began to be afraid of what the humans would say when the prime request would be asked. He knew all too well the anger of humans, and wanted to avoid anything to make the humans enraged; for he knew exactly how cruel some of them could be.

However, as the brave Dog has done in many a time past, in the protection of his home, his family, and the things he found dear to him, he began to speak. He spoke, not for the sake of speech, but to protect what was dear to him; which was the human, and the planet. Even if the humans didn't show that they even cared for their own well-being. He would still move to protect them from themselves. It was from this feeling, that he spoke.

"Lastly dear humankind, I seek to implore you of the prime request that we, as the collective animal kingdom seek to indemnify. We seek your help in coming to the resolution, that you will no longer utilize the planet's resources in such a way that is damaging to the environment for humans and animal species alike."

The entire audience of the assembly fell quiet. The Dog continued to talk.

"Many of the practices humankind exhibit, harm us. Knowingly or unknowingly, you even harm yourselves. We have a closer, more intimate view of the harmful effects of these practices. Many of the fish species call upon you to take care of the oil spills and garbage that humans now accidentally or

deliberately dump into the waters. Many fish species, complain that you do not value the importance of the oceans, and that if the oceans stopped performing their function, all of mankind would perish."

The general assembly members now in attendance began to whisper. Quietly at first, but then the whispering started growing louder. Louder still, as the Dog continued.

"Land species also request that humankind consider the impact of detonating nuclear bombs in the past, and how it has poisoned the earth, and of digging the earth indiscriminately for oil. The earth is poisoned, and this poison seeps into the land and the grass that grows is thus mutated, sometimes undetected by the human, and the animal consumes it and is mutated as well. This shortens our lives and is also the cause of the aggressiveness seen by various species, as they come into contact with humans."

To this, the people in attendance could not keep quiet.

"What would you have us do? Stop using *all* machines?"

They continued their outbursts.

"Furthermore, we use the same oil to protect your kind as well. If we didn't have oil, a lot of your stupid species would have died out a long time ago."

Such were the insults the Dog was made to hear. It did not stop.

"So what do you propose we do, since *you* animals are so smart and we humans are so destructive and stupid. Hmm?"

The Dog answered.

"Please do not get me wrong my friends. We do not mean to offend; nor do we believe humans are stupid or destructive. You are the wisest species on the planet, as God made you. We know that you use the gifts of this planet to survive. We merely mention the fact that these gifts are misused, and sometimes, the environment is not taken into account within such dealings."

People got angrier. Many started shouting insults at animals and some began to threaten. This is what the animals feared. The Dog cautiously looked towards the birds. They were getting ready to take off and tell the animal kingdom that the endeavor was a failure. He put up his paw to motion to the birds to wait a little longer.

"Please remember my friends," The Dog continued, *"my speech is not to offend. But we must present to you the damage that is being done, and what we must do to fix this. We only want the collective survival of all life on the planet to succeed. Should these ways continue, it would not only threaten us but also you. This is all we seek to portray."*

Someone in the crowd shouted out. "So what? Stop drilling for oil?"

"Yes, my friends, you must severely curtail this practice."

"And stop mining for coal or minerals? Or precious metals?" Said another.

"Yes, dear friends. I understand the need for such minerals, as many are used to make the medicines that treat illness, but you simply must decrease these methods."

"Nonsense!" A person stood up and shouted. "We know what is best! Not you!"

People began cursing and throwing paper towards the front. People were no longer listening to the Dog, but instead were having conversations amongst themselves, shouting that the animals were looking down on humans and that the animals were ungrateful.

Some accused the animals of wanting to cause trouble and were only looking out for themselves. The noise got so loud, that finally, the loudspeaker was turned on at the assembly, and all were asked to be quiet.

"We will have a one-day recess from the assembly, and return the day after tomorrow. The animals have had a chance to speak. Go and rest, and think about everything. When we reconvene, we will vote on this resolution in front of the whole assembly."

* * * * *

On the next day of the assembly, as all the representatives for the respective nations convened, the Dog was present, but none of his companions stood alongside him. The birds were to stay outside at distance, for if the Dog was attacked, or seized upon, they would fly away and spread the news of the failure worldwide. Animals would then know that humans do not care for an understanding.

The Dog, however, walked up to the podium and boldly entered the animal kingdom's greatest plea for mutual understanding. He spoke more eloquently than ever, imploring the need to make changes to how humans had thus operated and lived their lives.

Many, after some time to rest and think, had come to agree with the words of the now lone animal representative, and many came back and agreed openly with the animals and their case, and said they would work in their respective countries to come to an agreement and would vote to join the resolution of animals with mankind.

A few stated that they would engage, but needed to know that animals would keep their word and no longer attack, kill or maim humans going forward. Should a human fall into the water, larger species were asked not to pull them down underwater and drown them, but instead, to help them stay afloat as much as possible. The Dog mentioned that the dolphins already did this, but that he would spread the word to all fish species that they must all help as needed. They also asked that predatory animals, such as the Bear or the Lion would not hunt or attack humans, even if they wandered into their territory, but would ignore them and go their way. If there were humans who foolishly attacked, then animals would complain to the world, as they could now talk, and the offending humans would be tried in human courts and found guilty, as per the law. The Dog made the promise to the humans that they would spread the word to all animals that if any animal deliberately harmed any humans except out of self-defense, they would be put to death by the other animals or by humans immediately. To this, the reluctant humans agreed, and they all voted for the resolution.

This was a success. All animals the world over were overjoyed. Even the monkeys stopped making fun of humans and said that they weren't as stupid as they had thought. Animals around the world began shouting happily. The whole animal kingdom was abuzz.

After another day of staying near the assembly, and having further discussions with the respective representatives of the security council, the humans, along with the Dog, had worked out the details of the final resolution and was set to present the documents to the council for final signature and approval.

At the appointed time, however, the Dog could not be found in his resting area. There was a search commissioned by the assembly to inquire if he had gone home. As birds began to fly close to the area where the Dog stayed, they swooped down and began to yell and scream. They shouted for security to come. There was a large cardboard box near the garbage canister, close to the grass. As the birds gathered around, the security guard opened the box.

In it, lay the Dog, mercilessly choked and stabbed to death.

* * * * *

The afternoon of the next day, the news had broadcasted that the animals were planning to unite in mass. A bird, still loyal to the humans had shared the news that the animal kingdom would now confront the humans and demand answers to this act of senseless violence.

As the night wore on, many people saw long processions of animals, walking seemingly in one direction. Many feared for the resolution, and many feared there would be no understanding.

They feared there be might be a rebellion.

The Lesson

"Is it so bizarre to think that per chance, and this is a maybe, for we cannot know for now, but maybe, just maybe, Aliens don't really want to be near us? After all, what do we really have to offer?"

Humans had become able to travel far distances in space. We had not mastered the warp drive as yet, but we were able to accelerate ourselves a few times faster than the speed of light, all without dropping our mass. This was special because now we could propel large objects through space at astounding speeds. This was discovered in the late 21st Century. We had finally found the particle that allowed us to reconcile gravity with the other universal forces. It was a simple thing really, and it was present and abundant in nature all along.

The Oxygen atom.

Well, not the whole oxygen atom. We were able to collide atoms of oxygen with other atoms of oxygen, and instead of it producing O2 as we know it, the resulting smash created a small blast of finely broken mini O2 subatomic particles, that scientists referred to as 2-O.

I know. Scientists never really try with the names.

Anyway, in doing so, someone had the brilliant idea to collect these subatomic 2-O particles in a chamber, and combust them to see what energy it would release.

Here is where Newton and Einstein were proven wrong. This was a happy event for mankind, but sad for scientific scholars who studied the old guys. You know the thing. Relativity and all that. The 2-O particles had a strange behavior. Do you know the law of conservation of energy? That no matter/energy can be created or destroyed? Yeah, that was broken. The 2-O particles would burn, but before they completely released their energy, they would somehow quantum tunnel with another particle, and produce another 2-O particle on completion of release. Thus, the energy release never stopped, and as long as the particle was allowed, it produced a consistent, never-ending stream of energy without fail.

At first, there was a worry of the 2-O particles creating a chain reaction with Oxygen molecules in our atmosphere, and thus quantum tunneling out all of our oxygen, and then we would suffocate. This was disproven of sorts, as brilliant people posited that we couldn't run out of oxygen atoms, as trees produced a constant stream, and even then, oxygen was in abundance. Not like Helium. Thank God it wasn't Helium. No more floaty balloons? No more high-pitched voices on birthdays? The sheer horror. Supply was getting thin as it is. Amazingly, it was quickly discovered that the particles that quantum tunneled in unison with the spent particles, came from matter in the universe in regions infinitely dense, with infinite gravity, such as a Black Hole. So there was no cause for worry.

Hence, we had discovered infinite energy, a source of infinite fuel, and at the same time, broken physics. This was a celebration of great importance, because now, finally, we could achieve man's unbuildable project, the perpetual motion machine.

Many designs by scientists all over the world became possible and now worked, on account of our quantum tunneling 2-O friends. We starting producing electric cars, with a run time of you know, forever. We had unlimited energy. Energy became free. We no longer paid for it.

It's funny because before, we really couldn't destroy energy, so thus we couldn't create it. Hence, this is what made it so valuable; It ran out, or rather, we couldn't sustain the energy in its present state permanently. But now, we could, and of course, we wasted the stuff like it was water. People took trips to Saturn and came back home before dinner. Tell me how Mc Donald's was the first to put a restaurant on Mars? Ridiculous. I would have preferred a Wendy's.

Mankind could now propel themselves farther, longer, and carry more weight too. Thanks to the 2-O particle. Mass was not a problem. With the help of scientists, we abandoned Aluminum and other heavier materials for our spacecraft, and instead started using a combination of Carbon Nanofiber mixed with a newly discovered organic steel-derived isotope for a super-light, super-dense alloy that protected from micro meteor impacts. For our glass, we solved that too. Because we had unlimited energy, we sent large masses of glass in ships facing towards the Sun, and the sheer heat of the sun's radiation changed the atomic structure of the glass, and caused it to crystalize, then melt into the surrounding lattices of itself, and produce a clear impenetrable "Hyper Ionic Glass". Yes, again, with the stupid scientific names, I know, I know. Hey, I didn't name it. Don't be mad at me.

* * * * *

Since the solar system was colonized, it was decided that man would venture farther. The President just came back from vacation with his family, skiing on the icy slopes of Pluto, and we didn't have many more attractions. Neptune sucked hard. All the old people going there to retire when they found out the atmosphere prolonged life by an additional twenty years. Who wanted to hang out with all those old people anyway? You weren't even let in unless you were eighty and above. Ridiculous.

I was one of the astronaut recruits who was joining the mission to discover what was going on with Betelgeuse because she was starting to dim a little bit. We based our observations on this after we sent Hubble Hyper II to Pluto to observe her. She was looking sick. Scientists were a little worried that she was already dead, supposing her distance from us, so it was decided we would head there over a two-year journey, and find out, and then turn back towards Earth if we discovered a supernova blast coming towards our general direction.

As we lifted off, the perpetual engines signaled that they were running fine, so we unbuckled as we sleeked past the NISP, the New International Space Port. We had decommissioned the ISS years ago. Pile of junk. Can you imagine how stupid and useless that piece of junk was? Floating around the Earth, having astronauts pee and relieve themselves in bags. Disgusting.

Anyways, I decided I wanted to play some pool, so I activated the simulated gravity field and we got to have some fun.

As we neared Proxima Centauri, we got a new flight plan from the system AI, and it plotted a course slightly different from what it plotted on Earth. It identified an Exoplanet, about two months away from Orion's Belt, and it inquired if we wanted to go there to discover it. We thought it would be a nice show, so we agreed to the new course.

Six months had passed for us, and we radioed home to our families. I had bulked up and gained like ten pounds cuz I was working out like a damn prisoner. My wife was super impressed when I showed her my abs. She said she looked forward to being older than me when I got back. She said that when we left, NASA announced a new junior program for kids to learn to fly to the moon and back and that they were taking applications from children of astronauts first. They were developing the program to increase the pool of astronauts to someday send to faraway missions. I told her we should do it, and signed up our six-year-old son. He would be recruited when he was nine. He would complete the academy by eighteen. He would be so stoked to go to the moon and grab me some fries from the fried chicken buffet in the Lunar Super Walmart.

Trust me, the future is just as crazy as you think it *isn't*.

* * * * *

The rest of our trip went smoothly. I gained another five pounds and I was jacked. I had the female astronauts checking me out, but I didn't do anything. I was faithful. I swear.

As predicted, about two months from Orion's Belt, and Betelgeuse, we came upon the exoplanet. The AI in the ship recorded that it was slightly larger than Earth, and had nice purple skies. The AI then registered the purple skies as the chemical makeup of the reflection of the exoplanet's water. We asked how that was possible, as water reflects blue in an atmosphere. The AI said it wasn't sure, but that when we arrived. we should go down and take a small trip to investigate and collect a sample, and after testing it, perhaps it could tell us more.

As we decreased our speed, the planet came into full view. It was beautiful. It had a purple hue to it, and it shined from the reflection of its nearby binary stars. The planet sparkled. We took a sparecraft, and headed down.

Once near the planet surface, we began to register the most spectacular things. We saw Diamond mountains, and fields with flowers, their petals seemingly spinning on their buds distributing what seemed like purple pollen. Just then, we got a message over our intercom.

"We know who you are."

Our AI registered the sound, but reported that it wasn't coming from any one of us on the ship.

The voice began again.

"Stay the f*** away from us."

What? Who was cursing at us at a time like this? We thought it was some joke the AI was playing on us. The AI in the ship denied this and said the signal was coming from near the diamond mountains.

We changed course and headed towards the mountains. When we got there, we set the sparecraft down and got out. The place was beautiful. We couldn't believe the sight of the diamond mountain. It was so clear and bright, reflecting the light from the stars. We walked up to a small lake, and sure enough, the water was purple. We collected a sample in a small bottle, then headed back towards the ship.

Suddenly, there was a bright, intense flash of light, and I fell unconscious.

When I awakened, none of the other astronauts were around me, and I was locked into a strange curved, rounded seat. It felt flat, but at the same time, it was the roundest seat I ever sat in. It felt very weird.

The door opened, and in walked this tall guy. He looked just like me. Identical even. Like my twin. He walked straight up to me and slapped me as hard as he could in my face. I screamed out.

"Oh, you don't like being violated, do you? Huh?"

"What? Who are you? Why did you slap me? Wait, how do you look like me? Where is the rest of the crew?"

"They're back on the ship. You're going back as well."

"What? Wait, what? Why?" I asked.

"Because we don't want your kind or your species anywhere near us. Stay the f*** away."

"What? What's going on here? Why are you cursing at me?"

"Isn't that how your kind talks? Huh? Want me to slap your stupid face again?"

"No!" I said, "Please don't slap me again. Oh my God! What is happening? What is happening here?"

"*Calm down you idiot. I just projected an illusion into your brain to make myself look like you. I'm not trying to reveal my true form to your stupid species.*"

"Ok?" I said.

"*Ok indeed. Time to go back.*"

I was so surprised. I started asking the strange guy more questions.

"Do you live here? Who are you? What is going on?"

"*Ok, listen bud,*" said the guy, "*we don't want your kind here. You people f*** up everything you touch. Look at that shithole of a place you call a planet. Half your original species are already gone. Do you think we want you coming here and doing that to us? Get the f*** out of here.*"

"What? How?" I was so confused. "Can you please explain to me exactly…"

"*Explain what, clown? Your species are the garbage of the milky way. All you do is waste and waste. You finally discover perpetual energy and what do you do? You put a f***ing Mc Donald's on Mars. On Mars! One of your nicer planets. Why didn't you try that mess on Venus? Your kind should be ashamed.*"

"I don't understand…"

"*Nothing to understand, fool. Do you think we haven't stopped by? We've been watching you idiots for years. All you do is dump garbage everywhere. Does anyone on your planet even think about cleaning up your atmospheric junk? We had to increase the vacuum around your interstellar vicinity or else all that space trash you idiots put up there would fall back towards you and kill your stupid asses. Which in, we probably should let it happen too. That would teach you a damn lesson.*"

"Wait, you've been watching us?"

"*Are you deaf? I know your kind ain't the brightest, but now you also have a disability, fool? You heard what I said. We visited a long time ago. A few times actually. We meant to come and give your kind the formula for perpetual motion, and to show you how to turn carbon into diamond, without needing intense pressure and heat. But when we got there, you fools were fighting wars and bombing each other with your little firecrackers. What do you clowns call it? Fat Boy? Hilarious. My offspring could make a bigger bomb than that, and he doesn't even study the Natural Potents. We sat back and watched you. Then you accidentally discovered quantum particle tunneling. We knew you would soon branch out, so we got the hell out of there.*"

"Potents?" I said, "Wait, you mean the atomic bombs we dropped back in 1945? That was so long ago. What does that have to do with…"

"The Natural Potents, you idiot. Your kind calls it the Natural Law. Or what you refer to as "Physics". My kind calls it the Natural Potents. Try to keep up, fool. Yes, we saw your so-called "atomic bombs". We saw how you killed each other. That's when we decided we were done with you. Keep your planet, and go f*** yourselves."

"Why are you so angry buddy?" I asked. I stopped being surprised that a live alien was talking to me, and started getting angry that this guy was so foul-mouthed and abusive.

"We're angry because you got a planet with clear water. A rear specimen, even for us. Even in the Milky Way. What you got there in your little shitty bottle isn't water, you fool. It's our liquid excretion. It's just that our bodily waste doesn't harm our planet. It nurtures it. So, we spread it all over. Plus, you can't take that with you, it gives superpowers to humans, so I'm just gonna take that back now…"

"Wait, our pee does the same thing too in a sense. It has Nitrogen. Our urine nurtures the planet too…"

He slapped me again.

"Really? Are you trying to be funny? You idiots have water, and water has much more spectacular purposes. Purposes your species have yet to even fathom, and you waste and pollute it. I'm done talking to you. Time to head back, you clown. Oh, don't even think of coming back, or next time, my species will start smoking you for real…"

He then snapped his fingers, and I fell unconscious again.

When I awoke, I was on the floor, back in the spacecraft. The crew was standing around me.

"What the hell just happened?" I asked. "Did I just go through what I think I went through?

Another crew member jumped in.

"Did you talk to an angry, foul-mouthed person?"

They helped me up.

"Yes! I did! The guy was so angry and abusive! He slapped me twice! But then he started telling me a whole bunch of stuff about the Earth and the planet, and that they came by to watch us, and that we were fools, and all this crazy stuff."

"Yes! Same thing it told me!"

We looked at each other. We had just undergone a collective interrogation by an abusive Alien. The thought of how much of an asshole the Alien was to us, was however lost on our minds, as we instead began thinking about what he had said to us. As we left the exoplanet and headed towards Betelgeuse, we all had a sense of heaviness. A sense that despite the craziness of the encounter, the abusive alien was right.

The Line between Black and White

"This story was meant, to open the philosophical door,
To the realm of a specific miracle, but please be careful what
you wish for."

No one knows where it came from, or how it originated. It was a strange material. Some supposed it came from a fallen meteor, as it was found in a small crater, deep in the forest. It was discovered deep in the crater, and no plant life grew around the crater or the surrounding area near it. Some supposed it boiled up from within the earth. No one could say for sure. All we knew, was that it was found deep within the forest, as a clear, gel-like substance, waiting for the human race to find it, discover it and test it.

Discover it we did, and in doing so, we stumbled upon the greatest medical miracle of humanity's short existence; The Cure-All Drug. The Gel was first found and studied; its properties then reverse-engineered through gene editing and DNA reproduction techniques to make it suitable for the human body. Once the substance was synthesized for regular use, it did one thing, and one thing extremely well: It healed and cured *everything*.

Nothing escaped this miracle substance's reach. Cancer? Now gone. (To the collective gladness of the whole human race, I should add). Diabetes? Now a thing of the past. Heart Disease? No more. It was all gone. People were now living longer, prospering healthily, and generally, staying alive. People still passed away from natural causes and old age, and also died through unfortunate means such as accidents and willful acts of violence such as murders and manslaughter, but the common man no longer died of illness and disease.

If you were in the throes of end-stage Renal disease, or Stage IV Cancer, it did not matter to the drug. Once administered, it went to work, super boosting your immune system, fighting infection and disease, and strengthening the body's natural healing properties. It even helped the body synthesize new proteins, enabling the body to not only replace the dead tissues making up the damaged organs, but it also breathed new life into the metabolic rate and aerobic respiration of the human it was administered to.

Of such, the only known side effect of the drug was an extreme hunger and appetite. Old women, who once would eat a teaspoon of pudding once or twice a day, was now consuming steaks the size of eight-inch plates. Teenagers, suffering from anorexia, now ate three to four times their weight in food a month. Men, who were once sickly and had to drink down soup as their main sustenance, were now destroying full course meals for breakfast alone. It would seem that the drug needed immense stores of energy to work, and mitochondria could produce only so much ATP without requiring a large intake of food. The drug seemingly used ATP at an astonishing rate. As cell structures broke down within the cells, it just simply stimulated the body to create more cells, specifically rewriting DNA to create double the number of mitochondria per cell, thus producing more and more ATP to fuel its work.

The Cure-All drug was magnificent, but it was not perfect. One thing the drug was not capable of doing, was regenerating lost limbs. It was discovered that it could, to an extent, regrow a sliced off piece of skin or regenerate damaged heart, lung, and pancreatic tissue, but it could not regrow bones for some reason, neither could it remanufacture teeth. This was of little consequence though, as we always had dentures and prosthetics.

At first, the drug was secretly held under lock and key by the government, who deemed it some sort of "Super-Substance", healing the ailments of Politicians and government contractors and wounded soldiers who returned from battle. But after seeing these damaged, sickly men and women return home to their families, after being in their previous state, the rumors of the "Wonder-Drug" began to circulate. Soldiers would tell everyone they knew, even to the expense of their freedom, that there existed a drug that cured all disease and infections.

The government could no longer hold back the drug. It was sent worldwide to scientists the world over, for analysis and further testing. The substance was tested on all organic forms of life, with it working one hundred percent of the time on all organic living organisms, with the one exception, being plants. The substance seemed to have a slight effect on plants or trees, but that effect was one of slowing the plant's metabolism and ultra-violet utilization properties, instead of speeding them up. It did not disrupt the photosynthetic cycle, but it slowed it down considerably. This was an area of great contention among scientists and something they sought to understand, but they placed this on the back burner, for time was better spent analyzing the miraculous effects of seeing those afflicted with a previously incurable disease, now present themselves, fully cured and healthy, eating and consuming food like a horse.

For the unhealthy among us, life became worth living again.

People were seemingly freed from the demoralizing effects of disease and illness. Chronic conditions no longer plagued the human race. The drug, once it became available, was not allowed by greedy corporations to monopolize. Shockingly, it took all but one day for the whole world to agree that this drug should be for all humans. It was immediately passed into law, that all should have easy, cheap access to the drug, and that since it could be synthesized so easily, it was made available to all, over the counter immediately. This was done so easily it seems, as all races, all creeds, no matter your social or financial status, suffer from illness and disease. As we know, no one was exempt. Rich or poor, it mattered not, for if you developed cancer, it didn't matter how much money you had. If that cancer spread and progressed, you died, just like the poor. This was the main reason the drug was made available for all. Everyone could take this miraculous substance and benefit. Everyone could take the drug and live.

Everyone.

As previously mentioned, people were now liberated from disease. What was once a pipe-dream for some, held back by disease and poor health, became a reality. For some, this was a chance to now truly live. For others, it became the breaker of the chains holding back one of the cardinal vices known by all of humanity: Gluttony.

In addition to having to consume large amounts of food, people consumed large amounts of alcohol, never before attempted in life or theory. People smoked hundreds of packs of cigarettes a day, and only stopped when they ran out of money to buy more. Food was necessary to consume for the drug to work, but the other poisonous substances people ingested was not. However, the cure-all drug was abused to cure any ailments that followed from heavy drinking and full unleashed chain-smoking. People ate and consumed whatever they wanted. It did not matter of course, because the drug did its work. People were slurping down what appeared to be bowls of fat and cholesterol, but due to the cure-all drug, they lost weight. Most people slimmed down to their ideal body weight, per their genetic code, and simply stayed there, regardless of what they consumed.

The drug worked, no matter what. Some went as far as pushing the limits of the drug. Some would ingest poison and then take the drug to see if the poison or drug would win. People became just that curious and stupid. A few times the poison would win out, depending on the lethality of the substance, but most people were emboldened, for in the majority of the time, the drug would fight the poison and win.

Humanity had reached a new medical age. Science and Biology was actively booming, for there would be many, many experiments that could be carried out on people in relation to the drug.

Humanity as a whole gained a deeper sense of the amazing make-up of our bodies, and the structure of our genetic composition. New branches of Chemistry and Biology sprung up from these studies. So much new information came to the world, that many scientists took up the sole study of researching the effects of the drug on a single cell and made immense discoveries, enriching themselves and their families.

All appeared to be going well. The fear of hidden side effects began to diminish; for there was, for the most part, none. People were using the drug, it was working extremely well, and humanity had seen its last days of people dying from curable or incurable disease.

* * * * *

At first, all people were glad to get their sickly loved ones back in good health. Those who had lost loved ones before the discovery of the cure-all drug, lamented and mourned that the drug was not discovered sooner, hence they would have their family member still with them. These people were not against the drug, for it saved others, but still, they shared a sense of sadness and loss. As such, a day was made for all those people. It was called "The Day of Disease". Once every August 1st, The Day of Disease was celebrated as a worldwide holiday. Everyone stopped to recognize and appreciate the contributions to science and society by those who donated their life and organ to humanity for science. It was also a day to remember the lost loved one, who perished due to ailment and sickness. All people, of all nations observed this day, regardless of religious or personal beliefs. It was the one day where people remembered that it was not previously normal for people to not die from illness and disease. This day was respected by all, and as such, it helped appease the hearts of those mourning for loved ones who died prior to the cure-all drug's discovery.

* * * * *

As time went on, and people began to live much, much longer than statistical models could predict, the numbers started to change. The incidence rate of mortality among all races plummeted. As no one died from disease itself, the curve on all graphs and plot points dipped to nigh zero. Data statisticians had no recourse but to retool incidence graphs and charts to reflect the new numbers. Many charts and graphs became unnecessary. What use was there for a chart, depicting the prevalence of heart disease in the African American population, if there was none? What point was there to calculate the Cancer-related deaths of Eastern Europeans year over year? This was information no one needed or requested anymore.

However, seemingly within just a few months, a new chart was needed. This chart was not one that humans previously thought would be needed, and this, for good reason. The numbers were so mind-blowingly inconceivable, that no one would need to make such a chart, or plot such a graph. But alas, such an instrument was needed.

It was the *Population Chart.*

As people began living longer, it became abundantly clear that new models for population count and the number of people alive would be needed. The previous estimation of "slightly over seven billion" was now so grossly outdated, you were embarrassed if you still held onto such assumptions. The human population in just a few short months had now ballooned close to a mind-boggling nine billion people. This was of course, solely due to people living longer, and simply not dying from disease. For the most part, life could continue just fine. Cities saw their populations explode, but not within unmanageable outcomes. Most worldwide structures stayed in place, and the overall system expanded to accommodate the now increased participants in the global infrastructure.

The projections, however, are what became concerning. Future forecasts predicted models of population increase of fifty million a year or more as people now lived closer to a century, before dying of natural causes.

This led to many scientists warning of an overpopulation risk. Many laughed off the early sentiments, as people were all healthy, and no one was suffering. "Should this be a major cause for worry?" People said. Many even wondered why we still needed scientists, and others even purported that the scientists were now bored, since all disease was cured, and so they wanted to create a new "existential threat" for mankind.

But despite the warnings of the then scientists, the population rate continued to increase. Charts were even beginning to depict numbers not previously thought possible. A well-respected science journal released a new model population chart, measuring humanity no longer around ten or twelve billion in twenty years, but now at forty to fifty billion in twenty years. Such was the extreme projections scientists were making. And the scary thing was that,

These projections were all true.

* * * * *

As disease became a thing of the past, another unforeseen and remarkable thing happened. There was no need for an immense amount of hospitals anymore. Hospitals and healthcare centers, along with clinics and outpatient centers began shutting down at immense rates, all over the world. This coincided with the simultaneous collapse of the pharmaceutical and insurance corporations. As a result of this, Healthcare workers no longer had jobs to come to. Competition to obtain a healthcare position became extremely fierce. Those with specialties and skills that came in handy in regards to trauma due to accidents or shootings became the only healthcare workers in practice. For healthcare workers, the competition to hold onto and keep their jobs became so fierce, that people risked life and limb, or in one instance, even took life to obtain or keep a healthcare position. One man, desperate to hold his job, and not be fired from his position, stabbed a young man to death, after learning he would take his position and assume his responsibilities.

As healthcare workers began to be out of jobs and started to suffer in society due to lack of money to live and take care of themselves, the phenomenon came to be known as the "Null Disease Paradox". In it, you were a healthcare worker, trained to take care of and treat people who were sick and needed care. But now, the same healthcare worker was suffering, with no way to "cure" their "disease", for it was not a disease of the body, but a condition due to "lack of jobs in healthcare" that these people were now suffering from.

Healthcare workers became the new unwanted homeless. Indeed, who needed them? For those who were still young and had their young minds able to adjust and learn new skills and certifications, they turned to alternate forms of work. This was the only thing that saved them, for they could no longer make a living in healthcare or taking care of the sick. The older healthcare worker, however, was not so easily able to transition, for they had spent years, honing their experience, and performing their craft. Doctors, who were used to hundreds of thousands of dollars in salaries due to their field of work, now barely made close to nothing, only being consulted for trauma-related cases. Even then, the scope of such consultations was limited, for the cure-all drug made the curative work easy for those who remained within the healthcare system.

Many older nurses and doctors committed suicide. Too many, it appeared, suffered from depression under the Null-Disease paradox. Many took to alternate, shady methods to obtain money, including actual crime and robberies, and large groups of young, newly trained female and sometimes male nurses, now took to prostitution to obtain enough money to live.

In well developed, richer countries, the government took measures to help these now unfortunate people. Large packages of aid and help were disseminated to these affected healthcare workers, but it was seemingly not enough, for many billions of dollars were lost to the revenue of the healthcare industry and the government on a whole, as millions, no, billions of people no longer needed medical care. There was no longer a need for expensive imaging procedures, or ridiculously redundant cancer drugs and their insanely inflated prices. People no longer needed to pay several thousands of dollars per bottle of a drug that barely kept them alive. Hence, this money was no longer collected by the corporations and governments of these countries through the loss of taxes, and that loss in revenue was felt.

Even those who wanted to help the affected healthcare workers could not, for money was not flowing from people in need of medical care, but towards consumption. And consume they must, for humans now needed large amounts of food to satisfy the requirements of the cure-all drug.

* * * * *

It was a warm afternoon in August, just about a week after "The Day of Disease" day when a scientist began to run down the halls of his university.

He had been studying the effects of the cure-all drug on plants and was one of the scientific society's "outsiders" of sorts. His work was not particularly interesting, as it had been discovered that plants were not grossly affected by the drug, and organic life suffered no ill side effects. He was one of the few scientists still specializing in Plant Cell Biology that universities kept on, as a matter of function, with no real contributions to overall human knowledge, now that the cure-all drug was commonplace.

The cure-all drug, now in every facet of human society in the form of pills, injections, supplements, etc., was also now discovered in by-products of waste due to massive amounts of consumption. The drug was now even being tested and found universally in the global water supply. The substance was even found to survive the all-important Carbon and Water cycles, and subsisted in the earth and even fell with the rain. Many countries had simply added the drug to the water supplies of their sovereign states, and now it was disseminated to all parts of the globe and found almost entirely everywhere. All animal and plant life contained the drug. This was seen as a good thing because now the drug would even be as freely available as water itself. At the time, this was what was believed to be good. Little did we know.

As the man ran down the hall, his face was pale white, as if he had seen something so scary, it drained all the blood from his face. He ran and didn't stop running until he got to the head scientist who worked in the laboratory.

Upon seeing the Head Scientist, he began to shout that he needed to call a meeting immediately. The Head Scientist at first didn't realize the nature of the emergency, and as such, waved at the man to slow down and stop shouting. But the man didn't stop. He kept shouting. Many people had stopped walking and was standing, staring at the man as he breathed heavily, and shouted at the Head Scientist to call an immediate meeting, as what he just discovered was so important, that it needed to be shared right away.

The Head Scientist walked up to the man and touched him on the shoulder, and asked him to calm down and tell him what he had to say.

The man then took a deep breath, and as strongly as he could, he let out a single four-word sentence.

As some of the scientifically minded people, along with myself, who were there in attendance, understood the sentence and what it represented and meant, we all were taken aback and began to gasp. Some people even started to scream out "Oh my God!", for their intelligent minds told them the instant consequences of what the man had just discovered.

The man had uttered the scariest four-word sentence a man, nay, a Plant Cell Biologist could ever say:

"Plants have stopped photosynthesizing."

* * * * *

As the results of the scientist were checked over and over and validated as correct, a growing fear was now creeping up into the scientific community. The proclamation that plants had stopped photosynthesizing was one that many did not understand. After all, was not the trees and leaves still green and very much alive? Were we not still getting harvests and crops from our plants?

It did not happen right away. For the next four to six months, all appeared fine, and plants were producing their crops as scheduled. But things began to change. Suddenly, the majority of leaves on all plant life turned brown, then Black. It was now approaching early spring, but the trees who shed their leaves in the Winter did not regrow their leaves as expected. There was also little to no flowers anywhere. They were nowhere to be found. The bees also seemingly permanently disappeared.

In warmer climates, where there were no harsh winters, crops began to take longer and longer to produce a flower, much less, fruit. Many species of plant life, who flowered regularly, now withered and died, instead of regenerating and blooming as they annually did. For some trees, the leaves stayed green, but the majority of trees who still had leaves began to shed them. This was happening globally. Whereas a bean plant took only a few weeks to flower and produce beans, it now took six months for the plant to even flower. Many seeds germinated, sprouted, and shaped small leaves, using the energy stored in the pod it sprouted from, but then died the very next day, as they could no longer create their energy.

Stronger trees did not all at once shed their leaves, nor did their leaves change color. These were the pine species, and for a while, they remained green. Evergreens appeared to give humanity hope, for their leaves stayed green year-round. This was seen as a sign of something good, for we thought that plants and tree life would simply bounce back. These hopes were immediately dashed, for it was quickly discovered that these trees, in an effort to survive, were utilizing the stored nutrients in their massive trunks, and this gave the false appearance that the tree was sustaining the leaves and that the leaves would survive.

These discovered theories proved true, when shortly after, even the Evergreen, after it had depleted its internal resources, shed off all its bristles, and now without stored internal nutrients to sustain it, withered and died.

Grass stopped growing. Important staples such as Wheat, Corn, and Rice also stopped producing, as all photosynthesis had now ceased. This became a curious sight to see, for the sun was shining as brightly as ever, but plants and trees simply did not utilize the seemingly unlimited energy they once fondly took so much advantage of.

The problems did not stop there, for with plants not soaking up the majority of the sun's energy, the planet warmed even more. Furious storms and bad weather were experienced in areas with seemingly mild temperatures and warm, balanced environments.

Most people did not understand the scientific ramifications of these horrific discoveries, for they were simple-minded, and only knew things as they affected them. But even simple people began to understand. Certainly, they could not understand the innate intricacies of the elaborate and wonderfully complex process of photosynthesis in plants, but they understood quite clearly when the announcement came that there would be a shortage of carrots and lettuce and cabbage, and broccoli, and beans and all products of plants due to a cease in photosynthesis.

Scarier yet, what was not known to the simple-minded folk, was that not only would there be shortages, the food supply was in fact, running out. Plants were no longer producing the large crops they previously did, and mankind had doubled, no tripled its intake of food since starting to utilize the cure-all drug. Not only that, but livestock also suffered, as there was no longer enough grass available for them to feed on. Barn supplies of freshly dried hay for livestock feed was quickly used up.

Due to everyone's now increased appetites, we were now eating our way through our stored-up food supply.

Food banks and food storage facilities quickly began to deplete. It was of little consequence to plant new crops, for any new seed, once germinated and exposed to water containing the cure-all drug, stopped photosynthesizing the sun's energy and died.

People, in desperation, turned on the only other source of sustenance besides plants: Animals. Many animals started simply going extinct, as people, in pangs of hunger, sought out any other animal with any sort of worthwhile meat to consume. The horrid thing was, that the meat did not last long, because animals had grown thin themselves, from lack of good pastures and feed. People needed to eat large sums of food; indeed, large amounts of it, and carbohydrates and starches were no longer available. Most, for a time, subsisted on an all-protein animal diet, free and devoid of any form of plant roughage or composition. True carnivores.

As humans continued, notwithstanding, disease-free, people were eating massive amounts of food so that the cure-all drug could work so they, in turn, could remain free of disease. This was the new vicious cycle. Not only was this bringing on the food supply shortage, but it also caused humans to consume yet even more, for the goal was to stave off disease, and in the course of consuming bad meat, and ingesting unhealthy substances in the place of fresh fruits and vegetables, it caused the body to need to work more, to stave off disease, thus requiring more food.

Now, for the first time, people began to truly experience the pangs of hunger. What poor, under-developed children in downtrodden countries experience on a normal day to day basis, people all over the world were now experiencing. With more and more people staying alive, needing to eat, food became more precious than money. Millionaires happily spent a million dollars or more for a few extra bags of rice to hoard. Simple plain rice, now used to sustain their bodies, so they could stave off cancer. Simple oatmeal, now bought as happily as the caviar they once consumed, now gladly eaten, so they could stave off the hereditary heart weakness passed down in their genetic material. They would do anything to not get sick ever again. The money mattered not. For no matter how much you had, you realized a simple fundamental thing.

You could not eat money.

Governments the world over began attempting to hoard food, but it never worked, for even the ones who hoarded, needed to eat the thing they were hoarding just as rapidly as the ones who sought it. It became certain, that the global food supply would be broken within a matter of months, should something not be done.

Worse yet, a new, more existential problem began to present itself. While hunger gripped the world, few realized that we would be doomed even sooner, for plants did not only photosynthesize to feed themselves and give out its products in the form of fruits and vegetables, they did a much more important job than that.

Indeed, this one function was the sole function above all else, that plants photosynthesize. They do it, certainly to make their food, yes, but *much more* importantly so, to respirate, or in other words, to breathe. And what, may I ask you, do plants *breathe out*, that we, as humans, need to *breathe in* to live?

The Line Between Black and White
II

"What decision will Man, move forward to face? Such a terrible fate to choose, for it is a choice between a rock and a hard place."

As world leaders sat down in meeting with each other, it became the topic of discussion of what must be done going forward. This was no time to play politics or to draw out the conversation. They got straight to the point. Food was running out. Not only was the growing food shortage becoming more and more a reality, but they also began to realize the other side of the cruel coin: there were now too many mouths to feed from the little food that was left.

The population was exploding. Plants no longer gave mankind food. Oxygen levels were beginning to decrease.

It was decided then, that something must be done to rid the "cure-all" drug from the water supply, as it was the sole reason why plants had stopped photosynthesizing. This would not, by any means be easy, for the drug was now deeply embedded into the global water supply, and the Water Cycle itself. How could we get rid of the substance, if it even survived evaporation?

Scientists were now looked upon once more, for now, they were tasked to produce a "counter-substance" to the cure-all drug. This substance, once administered to the water supply, would reverse the effects of the cure-all drug in plants, and thus restart photosynthesis.

While scientists were absorbed with their work, the global supply of food and meat was dwindling at a rapid rate. The animals who remained were quickly consumed, and all that was left was few if any of the edible animals used for meat. The only thing keeping them from being eaten but for the sheer terror of making them go extinct. Now, people began hunting wild animals. For the wild animals, many went into deep hiding, somehow realizing that the human had gone crazy in their pursuit of them and their meat. Many species, despite those seeking to protect their horrifically muted numbers, still went extinct.

More than a year had passed, and now people, who did not have enough food to eat, were starting to break down once again from the effects of not having enough energy produced by food. The cure-all drug still worked, but now it couldn't function to heal the body, for there was now no large source of external energy being supplied, and the brain, through released hormones, directed the drug to cease its biological operation within the body, or it would damage the organs and kill the person from exhaustion. This was a human biological survival mechanism.

As the food supply began to get scarce, people now began to contract new diseases once more, as the drug would now lay dormant in the body, not being able to properly function due to lack of sustenance.

By this time, the population had already spiraled out of control. The population sat at a little over thirteen billion people, way more than what was predicted just over a year ago. This projection was even more extreme than what scientists could predict, for even elderly boomers did not die from disease, yet they needed to consume large amounts of food. As governments began to realize that this many people could not be sustained, devious plots of "culling" began to emerge.

* * * * *

It was reported over breaking broadcast news, that a particular country, known for its defiance against the world in continuing to threaten their neighbor with nuclear weapons, had, in fact, launched a single missile at one of its own cities, wiping out the entire population.

* * * * *

As world governments scrambled to figure out the cause of this horrific disaster and to ascertain the fallout for surrounding countries, and the growing reality of a pre-emptive attack to stop them from continuing this gross destruction of human life, scientists continued hard at work, applying all the knowledge they had obtained about the cure-all drug, to find a way to counter it. Countries were now getting desperate; the madness had truly begun. So far, no wars had been started, and despite the major food shortages and hunger, government and way of life stayed stable.

However, at the realization that a country would annihilate some of its people to "cull" the increased population, a new fear spread. "Should our government be trusted to protect us?". "We already have to worry about food shortages, will our government also kill us to decrease the surplus mouths that need food?". These were the questions that many people asked. Many governments assured its people they would never perform such reckless acts of violence on its people, and attempted to dissuade the public from panicking.

This was all but a farce and a show of false beneficence, as governments all began, in some form or another, to enact plans designed to kill off large amounts of people. In Europe, there were reports of a whole town's water supply somehow being "accidentally" poisoned by terrorists. Millions died, as they learned too late that the poison was an undetectable, odorless poison developed solely to kill in several days.

In America, the methods of "culling" became simple and elementary. America simply went back to its roots. The government, subtly at first, went back to treating certain races as second-class citizens, as having no rights to the common levies of man. For all intents and purposes, this wasn't really seen as something new, for this was always how it was for minorities and other races in America. African Americans were now treated as they once were in the civil rights era. Many died, fighting to protect their family from house invasion and robbery.

Once these atrocities made it to the news, it was passed off as a *"accidental"* death, spurned from an "innocent hungry raider", looking for food. But this was not so, for many were secretly armed by the military and covert government operations to naturally shoot and kill people found without protection or defense. Young Black men were constantly gunned down in the streets, simply just going their way, bothering no one. This was immensely infuriating to many, for we knew all too well what was happening. Nonetheless, these methods were never attributed to "population culling", in the innate sense of the word, disgustingly, but rightfully so, because this was what was happening before the cure-all drug was ever discovered.

The government agreed that it was indeed horrible what was happening to minorities, but argued that it was not due to a villainous or evil government plot to cull the population. I cry in my heart, because the government, while of course lying to the people at the time, had a valid argument, and I am inclined to agree.

If you disagree, I urge you, go on, make the case, and show me how I'm wrong...

* * * * *

As countries began to take to these methods to decrease the surplus population, many people began to rise to incite a civil war. Food and resources were worth fighting for, and so, people began organizing in small pockets at first, but then in larger and larger installations of people, with the intent to survive being "culled" by the government they lived under. It was designated a time around the world, where people all over, would rise to overthrow their respective governments when it was proclaimed that the "counter-drug" was found.

The news of the discovery of the counter-drug by scientists seemed to quell any ambitions of overthrowing of power for now. As scientists quickly disseminated the information they had and began to synthesize the new substance, hope seemed to creep back into the world. For a moment, people began to hope for a resolution to the dire state of mankind.

As the new substance finally began to be distributed and mixed into the water supply, plant life began to slowly spring back. Plants who were hanging on started to slowly recover in days. Trees that were on the brink of death, immediately started casting out leaves. Over the course of several weeks, all crops started producing fruits and vegetables again, as if nothing had happened. The seed bank, relatively stable, and thus so far secure, disseminated extra seeds for planting to make up for the loss of seasonal planting seeds. The stock was then quickly and respectfully replenished, as crops yielded.

As plant life recovered, food started making its way back to all areas of the globe. Not only were crops being harvested, it also seemed that plants were producing excessive amounts of the things they produced. Whole orchards were bowed to the ground with apples. Vegetables were growing abundantly; food was practically being given away for free. People started being able to eat decently again. People could now farm livestock once again, for grass appeared to grow back fervently, and people no longer sought out all animals for consumption alone.

Not only did the flowers return, but the bees also returned in abundance. In addition to this and to the viewing pleasure of many, the butterflies also returned in droves, lighting upon everything that shed a flower. The world became beautiful again.

Oxygen levels began to once again, stabilize. As trees began to collectively contribute to the atmospheric oxygen content, many areas with bad weather began to stabilize and experience good, mild weather once more. Everything seemed to once again stabilize and settle down.

However, as the counter-drug continued to work, people once again fell back victim to disease, and began to once more, with great sadness, die from illness, and disease-related complications.

People began having heart attacks and strokes again. The first incidence of lung cancer was once again recorded in people a little over six months after the counter substance began working. It became known then, that the counter substance was nullifying the effects of the cure-all drug.

People were dying once again from disease. In large numbers.

Many grew sick from eating all the poisonous substances they could, whilst on the cure-all drug. The population statistics once again began to shift back towards an increased mortality rate among those who heavily drank alcohol, or who exhibited excessive cigarette use.

Upon realizing what was happening, people began to immediately ask for the cure-all drug once more. This time, the drug was not so easily found and disseminated to the public. Rightfully so, for while the drug sustained human life, and rid mankind of longstanding, chronic disease, it also caused all plant and tree life to eventually stop photosynthesizing and producing food products necessary for human consumption. This not only broke down the food supply but it also greatly affected the animal kingdom, as many animals, who relied on the simple grass growing in the field, died of starvation.

Initially, there were protests. How could the government withhold a medicine that could cure their loved ones? How could a drug that could save my daughter or son's life be held back? Many people, who had sick family members and relatives, campaigned heavily to continue to use the cure-all drug. The scientists, along with the government felt that the drug, while it cures all disease, had too many existential effects at the cost of the human race, and as such, must never be used again.

Now, a new conversation was occurring.

Should mankind be allowed to continue to use the "cure-all" drug? Should humans forsake long term survival, and essentially risk or bring on immediate destruction for a short reprieve from sickness and suffering? Wasn't there anything we could do to mitigate the penalty of using the cure-all drug, while simultaneously shoring up our heavily relied upon food supply by all plant life?

Scholars discussed. Governments debated.

In truth, for many, there was no philosophical argument. The effects of the cure-all drug threatened the species as a whole, and even if it cured all disease, there would simply be no point, for the world would end due to lack of food production. Even still, if the human species somehow found ways to survive on a scarce food supply, it would instead suffocate from significantly reduced oxygen levels, as the earth would no longer be able to produce enough oxygen from the ocean alone, especially in the state we then had it, and frankly, *continue* to have it.

So then I ask you, what do you think; If you should thus come down with cancer, should you then die a painful, miserable death, while others live? Or should you be cured, but then, shortly after, as plants die once again, you risk starvation, suffocation, and destruction? Sure, your answer may be a noble one, for surely, people will see themselves as heroes and martyrs, and self-sacrificing for the greater good.

But now answer me this. Would you thus suffer your loved one such a fate of dying painfully from a now *easily* curable disease? To those who have watched their loved one suffer and die from incurable afflictions, and watched as they cried in pain and weakness, all the while wishing they could be whole again, yet laying on their deathbed, languishing in disease and squalor, wishing for just a little more time, nay, just one more day with their loved ones. Now time is thus re-winded, would you choose to sit there and watch them suffer all over again?

Suffer still, for weeks, sometimes for months on end? Could you then, give up your loved one to perish, in spite of how much you will miss them? In spite of the terrible pain and loss you will soon experience? For nothing? Knowing that you could have a few more precious moments with your mother? Your grandmother? Your ailing sister, or dying brother? Would you still let them suffer and die? Painfully and regretfully? I ask you.

Or will you too, campaign just like the others, to once again use the "miraculous" cure-all drug. Consequences be damned?

A Stranger's Visit

"This tale of the Stranger is simply not what you may think. Read every line, interpret ahead, don't blink."

O ne day, a middle-aged man had arrived home and opened his door to find a strange man standing in his living room. The strange man immediately told the man that he would not harm him and that he came just to talk.

The man, feeling very scared and threatened, ran out of the house and called the police.

When the police showed up, they went into the man's house and could find no traces of the intruder. The police told the man to call immediately if he saw the intruder once more. They also posted a car outside the man's house for a few hours, but no one showed up again. The police then left after a few hours of waiting.

The man called a locksmith and changed all the locks in his house that same day. He got an extra lock for the front door and even set up a camera pointed at the door to see if there would be any intruders trying to break in. As he was adjusting the camera, the intruder, whom he saw earlier, was standing behind him.

This startled the man so much that he screamed out and went to grab his phone. The man who was standing there told him not to be scared because he would not harm him, but the scared man, still not listening, reached for his phone.

As the man put his hand in his pocket, he looked up and saw that the stranger was holding his phone in front of him.

The stranger told him that he would give it back to him, but that he should not call the police again, because he didn't know how much time he had left, and all he wanted to do was talk.

"What are you, like the devil or something?"

"No, certainly not. Please calm down."

"How are you in my house? I changed all my locks!"

"Calm down my Brother. Don't shout. I didn't break in."

"What do you want with me?"

"I just want to talk to you."

"About what?" The man asked.

"A few things. But first, calm down. Here's your phone. I don't want to hurt you in any way, shape, or form."

The stranger slowly walked up to the man with his hands up and cautiously handed the man his phone. The stranger then walked away and sat down on the floor in the living room and asked the man to come to sit down. He assured him once again that he would not be harmed in any way, and that the man could trust what he said because he wasn't in the business of lying. The man relieved that the stranger seemed to genuinely want to talk, came and stood by the couch, but refused to sit.

The stranger laughed and said that the man was silly to fear him. He was neither dangerous or harmful to him in any way.

"Why should I believe that?" The man asked.

"Because I'm not. Don't worry. I couldn't harm you if I wanted to. If I did, I would probably be the one harmed"

"Ok? But this is my house. What are you doing here? Can you just leave?"

"Well, honestly, I could...but I won't. Not before I talk to you."

"Ok, alright. Talk, then when you are finished, kindly leave."

"Well, ok, but it will be much better for us to have a conversation, no?" Said the stranger.

"I don't know? Is it better?" The man asked.

"Tell you what, go, bring us something to eat, because we have a lot to talk about, and I know you have some baked mac and cheese in the fridge. Bring me some will you?"

"You're hungry right now?" The man asked, now slightly less threatened.

"Yeah. We can eat, then we can talk. Again, I promise, I will not hurt you in any way. If you feel better, I can even lay on my belly, let you tie my hands behind my back and everything. Well, maybe leave me one hand, will you? Unless you wanna feed me? I'm ok with that. Anything to make you feel safe."

"No, I'm not feeding you. I will get you something, but I'm watching you. If you make one move or try anything, I will call the police and grab a knife. Ok?

"*Ok.*" Said the stranger with a smile.

As the man went to the kitchen, he came up with the idea that he would call the police and tell them quietly that the man had returned.

As he reached for his phone, the guy shouted from the living room that there was really no reason to do that and that he should just bring the food so they could talk after. He said he should hurry, for he was very hungry and wanted to eat.

"How did you know I was gonna get my phone?" The man asked.

"*Please my brother, where's the mac and cheese? I told you I'm hungry, and you make good baked mac and cheese. Just bring me some please.*"

At hearing this, the man, still somewhat apprehensive, brought some mac and cheese for the stranger.

The stranger ate every last drop of the food he had on his plate, said it was good and belched. The stranger had made himself comfortable in the man's house it seemed.

"Ok, so now what do you want to talk about?" The man asked the stranger.

"Well, you tell me." The stranger replied. *"After all, this was all your doing."*

* * * * *

As the stranger stared at the man, he smiled and laughed a little again.

"So this is where you live huh?"

"Yes. So?"

"Well no, it's ok. I'm not judging. You do what you want brother."

"I'm not your brother."

"Well actually... The Stranger paused mid-sentence. Then he started speaking again.

"You know what?"

"What?" The man answered.

"You surprised me. I never thought you could pull it off. But here you are!"

"I don't know what you mean, guy."

"Yeah, you do." The stranger replied.

"No, I don't." The man answered again more strongly and annoyed.

"Hehe, Of course, you don't. Tell you what, I know this is rough for you, so I will just come out and say it. But I don't think you're ready to hear the truth."

"What truth?"

"Eh, I don't know. You were supposed to figure it out yourself."

"Figure out what?" The man asked.

"Well, aren't you the little conman? Aren't you? Trying to get me to talk. You were always a smart guy."

"Can you stop playing games and tell me what I was supposed to know? Or what I am supposed to figure out? The man began to get angry. "You come to my house, and hold me here hostage, then you won't tell me what you want?"

"No one is keeping you hostage, my brother. I just wanted to talk."

"Then talk!" The man shouted. He was a man of a short temper. He always had little patience for people who would jerk him around or played games.

As soon as the man shouted, he had a strong headache. It only lasted for five seconds, but during that time, he swore he saw a bright flash of light and what looked like a lot of white linen floating all over the place. He blinked, and it was gone.

"What? What was that? Did you see that?" The man asked.

"*What did you see?* The stranger replied.

"I don't know. It was strange. As soon as I yelled at you, I had a headache, and I saw a lot of white sheets and linen everywhere."

"*White sheets? White Linen?*" The man laughed. "*You saw white linen?*"

"Yeah, it was floating around everywhere. That was so weird."

"*You are too much, brother. The first time you recall something, you see white sheets. That's a good one.*"

"The first time I recall? What does that mean? Can you please tell me?"

"*Ok fine. Since you are taking so darn long, I will tell you. So listen, you did something.*"

"What did I do?"

"Well, I hate to break it to you, but you aren't human. Well, you weren't previously anyway."

"I'm not human?" The man asked. "So then, what am I?"

"Well, you are a..."

* * * * *

It had been now several minutes since the stranger had shown up in the man's home. He had eaten his food. He had made himself comfortable. He had laughed and joked with the man. But now, joking and laughing was for the most part, over with. It was time to get down to business. The news of what the man was, as told to him by the stranger, was met with silence and disbelief. Finally, the man spoke.

"Come on. Really? That's the best you can do? Huh? You expect me to believe you?"

"I'm not lying. I told you, I'm not in the business of lying. Besides, there are others who do it way better than me."

"I'm a man. Not a..."

The stranger interrupted him.

"How do you suppose I got your phone out of your pocket when it was still in your pocket? Hmm? Matter of fact, how did I get into your house when you changed the locks?"

"You're a pickpocket and a thief or a burglar. That's how."

"Now, now. You don't have to call me names. I told you I didn't do anything like that. I walked in."

"But how is that even possible what you said?" The man asked. I just can't be. I have lived all my life as a man.

"Well, you're not, ok? So just accept it."

"Accept it? Are you serious? You come here and tell me something like that, and I'm supposed to accept it?"

"Well, why not? Is that a bad thing?"

"Well, yeah! I mean, how am I...and what happened to cause me to...this is just all so confusing."

"Don't worry. For now, just accept it. We have to discuss some important things."

"Like what?"

"For starters, do you want to stay a man?" The stranger asked.

"What do you mean? Stay a man? Of course, I want to stay a man. What does that even mean?"

"Hey, I'm just doing what you asked."

"What?"

"You asked me to ask you if you wanted to stay a man when we talked next…so I asked you."

"This is insane and crazy. Listen, guy, I need you to leave. I'm done."

The man walked over to the stranger, and now, feeling confident and bold enough to touch the stranger, he reached out his hand to grab his shoulder to force him to get up and leave.

"No, wait, don't touch me so deliberately yet! You're not ready…"

As the man grabbed the stranger, the man experienced a second flash of light. When he opened his eyes, he saw the image of the white linen and sheets again, but this time, the linen seemed to be wrapped around people. As he took a closer look, the linen cleared up to be shaped like people, only bigger. They were all over the room, crowded. As he looked at one of them, the person, now seeing that he was directly looking at him, turned towards him. All the white forms did. They then started walking towards him. The man screamed and closed his eyes.

When he opened them, the stranger was standing in front of him, waving his arms in the air, fiercely, seemingly at the air behind him to move back. The stranger then said: "*Give him some space.*"

"Give who space?" The man asked, confused, and still scared.

"*Don't worry about it. Hey listen, I'm sorry. I should have warned you not to touch me yet. At least, not so deliberately. I knew it would cause you to see what you weren't ready to see.*"

"What was that?" The man asked.

"*You know what that was. You know exactly who they were.*"

"No, I don't. That was scary. Why were all those people in the room suddenly like that?"

"*Ok, so don't be upset.*"

"What is this? What is going on?"

"*I was trying to tell you before; you are not a man.*"

"Oh Jesus, what is happening? What is happening to me!"

The stranger cringed and slinked back a little. Almost as if in sudden pain. The man noticed it and stopped screaming.

"What's wrong with you?"

"Nothing. It's just…I can't stay here much longer, that's all. Listen, calm down, I promise, you are fine."

"No, I'm not fine. One moment I am seeing you, then the next moment, the room is filled with people in white clothes. Is this really true?"

"Yes. But listen, you have to make a choice now."

"What choice?"

"We need to know; do you want to stay a man?" The stranger asked.

"We? Listen, I'm freaking out, guy. Can you please explain to me what is happening?"

The stranger explained again.

"Ok, but if that is true, why would I do that?"

"Well, you said you wanted to see what it was like to live like a man and that you wanted to see how hard it was to live like that. You were simply given permission, and you did it."

"You mean, I "chose" to be a man? To be human?"

"*Correct.*"

"Who chooses that? No one can "choose" who they are. And why? Even if what you say is true, why would I do that?"

"*Because you said you had to know for yourself. So, listen, the time is almost up when you have to make a decision. Either stay a man, or...*"

"I want to stay a man."

"*Really? Despite what you just saw?" Aren't you curious to come back? At this point, if you did want to come back, you still can.*"

"No, I am a man. I was always a man. I don't want to come back. And come back to where? Where exactly would I be going?"

"*Huh. You think you truly know someone.*"

"What do you mean by that? You don't know me."

The stranger laughed. "*Of course, I do brother. Come on. Do you know how long we've been together? You're funny.*

Listen, I can't force you to come back, it has to be your decision."

"No, I won't "come" back. Or whatever you want me to do. Just please man, can you please just go?"

* * * * *

As the men conversed, it was growing later in the afternoon, almost getting dark, and the sun was about to set.

"Tell you what, I will let you see one last time. Don't be scared ok? No one will hurt you."

"Let me see? What? Just please don't make me see what I just…"

The stranger walked behind the man and touched the man on his back. As he did so, the man experienced another flash of light so bright, that he had to squint his eyes closed. When he opened them, an extremely large child-like being, twice his height, in white was leaning over him, two inches from his face, staring directly at him.

To this, the man startled and jumped back, right into the arms of the stranger who was talking to him before, but this time, the stranger had all over white on as well.

"Yes, my brother, you are one of us. See all these people here? You are one of them too. Come back with us. We miss you."

As the man turned around, he saw what looked like hundreds of people, all in white staring at him. He turned around in disbelief and rubbed his eyes as if to make sure he was seeing correctly. As he put his hand to his face, he blinked. When he blinked, he suddenly didn't see the whole white scene anymore. All he saw was the stranger, now dressed back in plain clothes, standing a few feet away.

"Did you finally see my brother?"

"This is crazy. This can't be real."

"I assure you; this is all real. Now, this is your last chance. You have to decide here and now, if you want to come back or no. If you do, you will finally get to see what this is all about. If you choose no, you will stay a man, and I will never come to see you again. Also, you won't remember this ever again."

"The man looked at the stranger. He was smiling at him so warmly. He almost seemed to have his arms outstretched as to beckon him to come closer. The man started walking towards the stranger, almost as if to decide to come with him when he stopped. He remembered that he just wasn't sure if this was all an illusion. Or if this was a trap? Or some weird dream?

He hesitated. Then he stopped walking.

"No, I just can't. This doesn't feel right."

"*So you don't want to come with me. You are choosing to stay a man?*"

"Yes. I don't know how real what I just saw is, but I know I am a man. I don't want to be something else."

"*This your final answer?*"

"Yes."

"*Ok. As you wish.*"

The sun had just set. It was now getting dark. The outside night lights began to turn on.

"*The time has now passed. You will stay as a man.*"

"Ok, now can you just go?"

"*I'm already gone. Take care, my brother. In my opinion, you have chosen quite p...*"

As the man turned around, he wondered why he was standing alone in his living room. He went to the kitchen to find the fridge door open. He wondered if he had gone to the fridge to get something and forgot to get it.

* * * * *

"What was his decision?" One of them asked.

"He chose to stay and wallow with the fallen beings."

"He chose this?"

"Yes."

"He can suffer and die with them then."

"Yes, but unlike us, he now gets a chance."

"Wait...a chance...Oh yes. Of course."

"Yes. It seems he made the right choice."

"Had he come back; he would be doomed like the rest of us. But since he stayed a human, he has a chance, a chance for forgiveness."

* * * * *

After they were all thrown out, of the countless zillions of them, one of them came back, imploring that he made a terrible mistake and that he knows he should not have taken the other side. He left the rest of them alone and did not join in any plans to cause Man to fail. After Adam's fall, he implored that he had had nothing to do with it, and begged for mercy, asking to live and be as the humans were for all time until the final punishment should come.

He sought to be allowed to become a human and stay a human. He said he would live his life the same way and suffer along with them, for he preferred to live this way and share the small light of joy the humans felt when living on the earth and embracing God. This he felt was so precious, as the alternative would be to keep the company of him, who caused all this, and this he refused to do. Also, he would be adamant and careful to never join the wrong side ever again.

He was granted his request.

God would not permit him to suffer in perpetual torment, as some now believe God does or will do to any created being. He would instead, live lives of human joy and suffering over and over once each for six times, then once more, for the seventh time. After this, he would then die and cease to exist, all without knowing the truth of his origins, as his memory was removed from him. God would then decide the fate of his now mortal soul, based on how he lived as a human, and not for the decision he made to rebel the first time.

His "Brothers" were some who wanted him to come back, but he ultimately made the right choice to stay, as God had placed him. He reasoned that this was better than the fate now awaiting them, as he dreaded the final punishment, and did not want to die this way. He still very much, loved God and wanted to show it through this act of repentance.

God, in mercy, spared him the final punishment and allowed him to live his remaining time this way. Six times, a fallen angel came to him to get him to turn back into an angel, and six times he refused, unknowing of what fate he would have in store for him should he agree. However, he successfully denied them each of the six times, choosing to stay a man. The fallen angels became jealous and struggled to do everything to make this once angel come back to their side, but they were always unsuccessful. Did God forgive him? Would he get the privilege of the sacrifice? The privilege of redemption? This was not fair they deemed. Nonetheless, these questions would not be answered for them, for they were no longer allowed to disturb or bother him again. After this, there would be no more indeed, for this was his seventh time.

* * * * *

The Amazing Opportunity

"A simple tale of a frightening look, of flattering words, of writing a book. Who, from lacking in knowledge may think they see, a fantasy of grandeur, an amazing opportunity."

O ne day, I won a short story writing competition, and as such, I was notified that I would get a small cash prize, and meet with a prominent writer and get tutorial lessons from him. As I was going to meet with the writer, I saw one of my favorite celebrity singers, walking down the street with her boyfriend. I saw them and recognized them instantly and was happy to see them, so I waved at them. I didn't want to make a fuss, because they were walking in broad daylight, and I didn't want to make a scene and get them dangerously rushed by onlookers and other fans.

Her boyfriend saw me and nodded to me as I was walking by. She saw me too, but she just smiled and they both kept walking.

It was nice to see them both, walking in public.

As I got to the writer's place, I stopped to buy a train ticket to get back home. Once inside the building, I was brought upstairs, and the writer was waiting for me, smiling at me and asking me if I found the building ok. I told him I did, and we sat down to talk.

I was offered something to drink, but I declined, as I had eaten breakfast that morning, and didn't want to be too full. I was also very excited to hear what this prolific writer had to say to me. Was my story good? Did he like it? What pointers would I be given? Should I be more creative? All these questions were floating through my mind, when the writer suddenly asked me, out of the blue:

"So, how much do you charge for your story?"

I was slightly confused. I at first didn't know how to respond and instead kept looking at him and smiling back.

He then repeated his question.

"How much do you charge for your stories?"

To this, I answered back in question form. After all, it was a confusing statement to me.

"Charge?"

"Yes," He answered. *"How much do you charge?"*

"Well, I have never charged for my stories," I answered. Still very much confused.

"Well, you should think of a price," He said. *"Because I want to pay you for the rights to your story."*

"Wait, you wanna pay me for my story?" I answered. At this point, the idea that was forming through my mind was that perhaps this was a test. Or perhaps, this was what a writer should think about, for if their story is good, people may want to discuss publishing it and selling it in bookstores, and publications, and all sorts of excellent other...

"Well yeah. Didn't they tell you what this meeting was about?" He answered.

"No, I thought I was here for a tutorial lesson on improving my writing."

"No, no. Your writing is fine. Actually, its more than fine. It's good. Really good. That's why you're here. I saw your

story in the writing competition, and when I read it, I sent a copy to my publisher to read it, and they agreed it was spectacular. I also have a producer friend who read it and wants to turn it into a movie or tv series."

"Oh wow! Oh wow! That's excellent! That's awesome!"

I was so happy and surprised to hear this. I felt like I had just won the lottery. I had won a simple short story competition, but now I was hearing from this prominent, prolific writer that they loved my work, and they wanted my work and the rights to it...

"So you need my story to make it into a movie? Oh, but you want to buy the rights to it?"

"Yeah. We want to buy the rights from you. How does a thousand dollars seem?"

"I don't know! I guess it seems great!"

"Awesome. All I need you to do, is sign and initial on some paperwork I prepared, and once you do, I will send you a thousand dollar check in about one month, as I don't have the funds now, but once this deal starts working, I will get you that money right away."

"Ok, sounds great!" I was super flattered. I mean, who has this once in a lifetime opportunity? No really? Who gets their book turned into a movie, much less, a simple short story? This was like the best luck I had in my life. Second only to seeing my favorite singer walk right past me. As I was thinking this, the writer went over to his desk and grabbed a stack of paperwork, not too thick, with little yellow tabs stuck all over. He said those were the places I needed to initial or sign.

I took the stack from the writer happily and proceeded to print my name and input the date on the first page. As I was inputting the date, he said,

"Don't forget to read through it, but don't worry if the language is complicated, it just means the deal will go through much more smoothly."

I nodded at him and began to read through the stack of papers. It was so authentic and official! One page said:

"I do hereby thus, on this day in two thousand and twenty, do hereby relinquish all my right, possession and identification with and of, indemnifying myself as not of composition or author of the selected work below henceforward, and transferring this established written work, with full

copyright and use to the new author as outlined on the last page"

That was the most fanciest set of words I had seen put together. This thing was legit.

As I was reading through, I started daydreaming of making so much money from my story. I would be able to take care of my family. When my story became a movie, I would tell my family I was gonna be rich, and that we would be ok from now on.

As I kept reading, however, I came upon a strange set of words. It had to do with royalties and such forth, as laid out in the document:

"No royalties shall be thus paid to the original author of this work, who in a direct and clear mind, is transferring the full copyright work. The author agrees to relinquish all right to royalty henceforth and forever..."

I looked up at the writer, who was sitting across from me, with his legs crossed, sipping a small cup of coffee, smiling at me. I asked him what that paragraph meant, for I thought I was entitled to royalties, after all, it was *my* story, *my* idea.

"No my dear," He said. *"That is the reason I am paying a thousand dollars right now. For complete rights to*

your work. You are completely giving it to me, and I will then send it to my publisher and producers to make it into a movie."

"Oh, I thought I was gonna get royalties after the book was published, or the movie was made."

"No, silly. The book will be mines. The movie will belong to the studio. We just need your idea and how you wrote the work. It is so unique, that if we change any elements of it, it won't be the same. It must be the work how you wrote it."

"Ok, but I am sad to know I don't get any royalties. I thought that was how it worked?"

At this, the smiling writer stopped smiling.

"No, if we buy the rights, we keep the product. Do you know how many things go into making a movie?"

"No, but I see the credits, so I know it is a lot of people who work on it."

"Exactly. It's not realistic for you to want to have royalties here. Ok? Just finish reading and sign and initial, and we can do the rest."

At that last statement, something of an alarm went off in my head. This didn't feel right. I was now starting to feel rushed. Something in my mind went off like a warning. The writer was looking at me, no longer smiling, no longer sitting back. He was sitting up, his hands clasped at his lips, looking at me, almost as if to try to figure out what to say to me next. I don't know, but at that point, I put down the paperwork and told the writer that I was very flattered, but that I needed a little time to think. I asked him if I could call him back in a few days to talk about it some more.

To that, he got upset.

"*No, you need to sign this today, or the deal is off. Do you know how lucky you are to get an opportunity like this? Me? A writer of my status talking to you, an unpublished author about wanting your manuscript? Do you even realize the depth of this amazing opportunity?*"

"I do, sir, I just don't know about signing away my story without getting nothing in return."

"*Didn't we say we will be paying you a thousand dollars?*"

"I know, but just that? I don't want to come off greedy, and I am truly grateful you like my story, but I just thought that the author of the work *usually* gets recognized, like J.K Rowling, or something. I don't see how someone else can take *my* work and use it as their own."

"We are not taking your work, we are paying you for it."

"I know, but even then, just one thousand dollars? Plus, you don't even have the money for me today. You will get it to me in a month. I don't know. This just doesn't feel right."

Seeing then, that I was now too apprehensive, the writer then got up, and stood over me, and took a deep breath in, and said to me that if I didn't sign this today, he would make sure no one saw my work again.

"Why would you do that?" I asked. I was so surprised. This writer now looked completely different from what he first was. Now, a towering figure over me, trying to get me to sign away all my rights to my work, with no sign or hint of royalties or payment, besides a measly thousand dollars.

"I can't sign this today," I said. I need to think about it."

"Just leave." The once smiling, welcoming writer now said to me abruptly.

I didn't wait to hear another word. I got up, with the paperwork in my hand, and walked towards the door. I intended to show it to some people to see what they thought about this contract I was given to sign.

"*You can leave the paperwork.*" The prolific writer said. "*You can't take that.*"

I turned and looked at the writer. This prolific, prominent writer. I then wondered, how many stories did he *actually* author? How many works that he previously published actually *originated* from him? I dropped the contract on the ground and quickly opened the door and walked out.

As I was walking in the street towards the train, I got a call on my phone. I was so surprised and distraught, but I answered it anyway.

"Hello," I answered with a sad tone.

"*Hi there, I'm Julie, with the Up and Coming New Author's Short Story competition. I wanted to reach out to you to see when you had available time to meet with the writer who will provide you with writing tutorials to improve your writing and see how you would like to collect your grand prize.*"

Part II

The Lyrical Poems

"Eternal Inspiration, I humbly come,

Seeking your *guidance* of what I may produce,

a literary work meant only to seduce,

the passing reader…"

-From, *My Noble Intention*

Introduction (The Lyrical Poems)

Poems are for me, a song that you do not need to sing out loud. I use them to express the inner workings of my mind, but to compose it in such a way that there rings a melody to it. If you read my poems in this light, you almost begin to sing along as you read. I am a big fan of the rhyme; if you use it correctly, the reader enjoys the structure and standard of your verse, similarly to a song composed for your ears. You can make it fun or sad, all while telling a story. I love writing poems with emotion. I love *reading* poems with emotion. Raw emotion fuels my writing.

Similar to actual prose, I like the concept of poems because you can give the reader a glimpse of not only your story as you want to tell it, but you can open a window to the actual emotion you are feeling, and immortalize it forever, all in short verse. My mother was a poet at heart. She loved to write religious poems. As I grew up and studied the works of some of the famous poets, I realized the value and strength of religious and spiritual poems. This too, is a type of song, indeed figuratively and literally so, as many religious poems have been transformed into uplifting, encouraging, faith-based hymns.

A person reading your poem gets a chance to experience the emotion you feel. That raw emotion, now there, paralleled from your personal thoughts, is set there for the reader, nay, the world to find.

And through interpretation and application to oneself, you may experience what the poet felt. Thus, you convey your feelings, all without having to sing or say a single word out loud. The reader need only read your words, placed down on paper, waiting for a chance to transfer these awaiting emotions, to their minds.

Poems by Me

A Descent into Madness

A Descent into Madness, of sane ponderings to bed, for I cannot yet control, the thoughts in my head...

I fear I lack control of my mind.

Cursed with intelligence, I share a glimpse, of the empathizing feel, The Song of dissonance,

A mark of a disorganized consciousness.

To escape what is real, to contend against the proof, I struggle to embrace the signal truth,

That my mind prefers to misbehave.

Each and every voice, independent and strong, fighting for a chance to prove me wrong,

I fight an unceasing, endless war.

The journey from what is real, to the destination of
what is not, a small Black stain, a failed inkblot,

A place where fantasy becomes the truth.

The voices I hear, each vying for space, my sanity
forgone, for they seek to replace

The tepid line of the fourth dimension.

I descend into chaos, I am bound by the chain, the
battle is lost, hence I struggle in vain,

To fix the unfixable vessel.

The Time has come, for a glimpse in the face, the
mirror of myself, the penitent embrace,

The realization that I've lost my mind.

A Moment in Time

A moment in time, a single second to place,

I am in awe of your kind and pretty light face.

I see no expression or countenance like yours,

Your kindness spilling forward, it flows and it
pours.

A moment in motion, a swish of your hair,

Your smile, so soft, so warm and tende're

I reach to touch and smooth it away,

No words to express what I want to portray.

A moment in life, we were fortunate to meet,

So close, so far apart, to grow and compete,

Space shared with the common, and the future
elite,

Hearts wondering close, a developing fondness to entreat.

A moment of struggle, many of this to be had,

Our backstories in time, with some of it sad,

To see us apart, some would simply be glad,

Still, we stick with the good and reject all the bad,

A moment in the future, A risk not to be,

Guided by providence, waiting to see,

A simple defining moment, a transfer of trust,

Heading towards the next station, we're taking the bus.

Fearless

Where does it come from? How do you get it?

That spark that makes you fearless?

From the beginning, entering with high morale,

Nothing could touch you.

Each with silent sufferings known only to them,

Your horizon open to a future view.

A talk of your pain, your lack of financial gain,

Each different, but all the same.

Lord knows it isn't easy to maintain.

So Where does it come from? How do you get it?

That strength that makes you fearless?

Work piled on work, the body offended,

But nothing could break you.

So much more than what was expected,

Your determination pushing through.

The Days so cold, lives put on hold,

So hard at times, but going on bold,

Each and every one, a different story to be told.

Now Where does it come from?

How do you get it?

That light that makes you fearless?

Is it due to your promise? Your Amazing Potential?

We being here not accidental?

Strength shining through, to endure the pain,

Dreams of the future making it influential?

Success earned is never one dimensional.

So Where does it come from?

And how do you get it?

Yes, the ability to be fearless.

A struggle for hope, A reason for why,

To yourself you commit, you never lie,

Never surrendering to doubt, never choosing to die.

For it comes from the thirst, the quest for your need,

The light of your hope, the fight to succeed,

It was there all the time, you just had to believe!

My Noble Intention

Eternal Inspiration, I humbly come,

Seeking your guidance of what I may produce,

a literary work meant only to seduce,

the passing reader...

This, my forlorn attempt to entice,

Lyrics of song, meant only to suffice,

The common believer...

Yet, fearful in the attempt,

To display the thoughts of my Invention,

Of words strewn together,

My Noble Intention,

To draw you into my world.

The confidence I lack,

In bondage, I am held,

I sit nervously aback,

Watching my doubt and distrust meld,

For these words, inadequate, may be.

But I take solace in hope,

of future interpretations and dreams,

A silver lining itself.

A solace indeed,

That above all else,

I am truly freed,

From the bondage of my doubt,

The mistrust of my creed,

Hence, I go where you may lead.

Please guide my intention,

For it is noble indeed.

Qualities of God

Slow to Anger, Swift to bless,

With Abundant Mercy,

And Faithfulness.

Never-ending Goodness,

Unconditional love as proof,

Also Abundant in Truth.

Compassion of heart,

Understanding of Pain,

The True Breaker of the Chain.

A Lover of Life,

A Listening Friend,

The only One whom your heart can mend.

Infinitely strong,

and Infinitely Wise,

Someone who never, ever lies.

Keeper of your trust,

Abounding in Good,

The One Who always understood.

A caring Father,

Loving from the start,

The owner of the Biggest Heart.

The Light of Life,

With the Cover of a Dove,

The Habitation of Unceasing Love.

Things Could Be Much Worse

Things could be much better,

But Things could be much worse.

You just went and lost your purse.

And this tale begins with all, but mirth.

You were walking along the way,

With your shiny new purse,

And you slipped and fell on your knees,

spontaneously of course,

And the shiny new bag? Flew across the ravine with force.

You got up, took one look, and then you cursed.

Things could be much better,

But Things could be much worse

This story gets more unfair, this I truly assurs't

That scrape on your knee you started to nurs't

As clumsy as you are, you lost your purse.

As you get up off the ground, with yourself you converse,

How to reclaim what was lost, the reason for your outburst.

You then stop the shout, as you begin to feel a'curst,

For your throat is sorely dry, and you're dying of thirst.

Things could be much better,

But things could be much worse,

A car just hit you, smack dab in the hearse.

A slight bump in the rear, nothing to worry inverse,

But it certainly and magnificently very much hurts.

And yes, you still don't have that expensive purse.

So you scream and kick the driver, in the middle of his inner-wurst.

Yes, things could be much better,

But things could be much worse,

Your husband just texted you, that he wanted a divorce.

And that diamond ring he bought you, years ago of course?

Yeah, it was sitting right there, in the piddling purse.

A sad state of affairs,

It certainly couldn't get much worse,

"This is starting to get a little unfair," you think,

As you study your recourse.

So yes, things could be much better,

But things could be much worse,

You had your last twenty dollars in that forsaken purse.

How do you get home? You wonder at first.

But now that worry leaves your pondering hurst.

For like a strong wind, you let out another long curse,

As you remember the winning lotto ticket you had?

Sadly it sat in a side pocket, pretty deep in the purse.

Indeed, things could be much better,

But things could be much worse,

That ticket you lost? Now you're poorer than the durst.

Things are looking bad now, I must confess the worst,

The question behind it all, yes, this is the source,

A simple question indeed, an inquiry in verse,

Just why did you have to bring, that 'effing purse?

So you throw your hands in the air, Tis' bad luck you begat,

Then you sank to your knees, on the ground you bowed flat,

Oh! Did I forget to mention? You just knelt on a dead rat.

Its guts spewed forth, a simply horrid fact,

Some went into your mouth, and that was that.

I see that things could be much better,

But I say, things could be much worse,

You suddenly remember your phone wasn't in the purse.

You get to your phone, as a last recourse.

You would call someone to help, this you longingly yearn'st.,

but alas! the phone dies, in the middle of your verse.

Such a sad state of affairs this was, of course.

You forgot to charge the battery, Isn't that the worst?

Your eyes get watery, tears start to come forth.

Alas, things could be much better,

But things could be much worse,

Imagine all this happened at the same time? this was truly a first.

Now you're kneeling there in rat guts - dying of thirst,

Plus, you got bumped by a car - right in the hearse,

your husband decides to leave you - he wants a divorce,

you have no money left - with no recourse,

And yes, this all started cuz you lost your purse.

I can't really blame you if you felt a little be'curst.

Still, things could be much better,

But things could be much worse,

It's not the end of the world, so don't be so terse.

Life will go on, get up off your hearse.

Start walking towards the next station,

Forget the purse.

Go clean yourself off, go wash inside your mouth,

Those slimy rat guts, they're starting to swish about'h.

Borrow a phone. Go on and make a quick call,

You had a terrible day, but it happens to all.

Things could be much better,

But things could be much worse,

You are now home safe, in your Homesturd'st.

Safe in your home castle, the place of your birth.

There awaits your little Dog, Sally who greets you at first,

She is the only one who appreciates, your forsaken worth.

Hence you turn on the set, to take your mind off the day,

Shock of all shocks! What does the television relay?

A homeless woman on the news, standing in torn black tights,

Had found a purse with plenty of goodies and coveted delights.

A winning lotto ticket, and a diamond ring of course,

And twenty dollars to boot? what good luck had sprung forth!

Certainly, things could be much better,

And things are certainly much worse,

You really should never have brought the damn purse.

You begin to cry, as you stomp on the floor,

You are husbandless, jobless, unfortunate and poor,

Wow, telling this story has been such a chore.

I told your story, and it was indeed a good lore,

But now I quoth the raven, just this once, but "Nevermore".

Suddenly, you look up and hear the door,

A knock from the landlord, you owe him much more.

So things certainly could be much better, and they were before,

To tell you the truth, it's beginning to get very sore,

For you indeed, for bad things are in store.

Things could be much better,

But indeed, things are much worse,

You finally understand how much trouble It caused,

after you lost your purse.

So dear friend if you walk,

please stay on the course,

Don't be like our friend,

who went from good to worst,

Transformed from a joyous, and a happy life befors't

Now a cautionary tale, a sad sack of remorse.

I've Lost My Light

I've lost my light, it was precious to me,
I've lost my light, I am now blind, I cannot see,
I've lost my light, it helped and guided my way,
I've lost my light, dark now replaces, what used to
be day.

I've lost my vision, I stumble in the dark,
I've lost my direction; I don't know where to start.
I've lost my touch, I cannot now hardly feel,
I've lost my taste, nothing seems right, nothing is
real.

I've lost what is good, I struggle for the truth,
I've lost my conscience, the guidance of my youth,
I've lost my strength, I now struggle in vain,
I've lost my emotions; I now suffer in pain.

I've lost my sleep, visions of you, in my mind,

I've lost my dreams, A bittersweet trick to find,

I remember you now, in your past written word
and song,

I've lost my light, it was here, but now it is gone.

Were You Not Once Young?

Were you not once tenderly and brightly young?

Or from the bowels of the earth, you once had
sprung,

Like a seed, whose flower will soon now bloom,

Towards the sun, like the harvest or the fruit of the
loom?

Were you not once beautifully and gorgeously
young?

Like the melody a bird to the morning you once
sung,

Flying happily as the pollen-laden, circling busy
bee,

Or the Passion tearing all asunder, like the roaring
sea?

Were you not once loudly and insightfully young?

Silenced by the voices of those with leading
tongue?

Now a break from youthful awakenings, a cease
from my chant,

Seeking to march me in line, like the worker ant?

Were you not once hopefully and remarkably
young?

Rising in potential, your life is begun,

The future, you realize is there for your gain,

Of abundance and hope a 'plenty, like the pouring
rain?

Were you not once rightfully and decidedly young,

The awaited promise to which you first had so
clung,

I ask you to prove, you can know what I see,

How can you then, not try to understand me?

Were you not once verdantly and dazzlingly young,

The strength of your age, the hope of which you
hung,

The future's embrace, shining bright as the sun?

Were you not once hopelessly and wondrously
young?

Out of Bondage

Out of Bondage, we have opened our eyes to see,

Visions of freedom for all of us.

For a time, we were spared from bond and whip,

Set free of the chains that binded us.

Long have we waited, and long have we prayed,

Our joy, for now, it escapes us.

With hopes of freedom and joy, we would walk,

Free from the ones who would berate us.

We seek that freedom, with all our hearts,

Our tears flow down from within us,

We cry at our new bondage and the new chain,

We despair at the law that mistreats us.

Wait yet we must, for despite the terror;

The injustice of the murdered among us.

Our disbelief only silenced by the quiet rage

For we know that it is because they fear us.

Yet our rage spills out, for the innocent die,

This happens to the best that are among us,

An animal to put down, to torture and kill,

For this is exactly how they truly feel about us.

Still, we struggle, as keepers of pain,

The blood, they spill, that leaves us,

Gives life to the same folks who would seek to try

To make every effort to defeat us.

No parent should see, no person witness,

Screams in throes of pain, right before us,

Yet they do it, for they know they will simply get away,

By the lie, the blame, the system hostile towards us.

Justice demands an equivalent price,

Yet they pay not for crimes committed against us,

Despite the fact, we fought for our place,

Just as you, in the Civil War, right alongside us.

Comes now the time, they bring the cruel gift,

We have not freedom to breath in the air among us,

It is one where they seek to lay down upon your neck

To torturously kill you, through *hypoxia,* is what they bring us.

For we have come to know, the present truth

What reason do you have to hate us?

As if only our race contains the evil gene?

Or is it pleasure you seek, when you betray us?

Us, they hate, but we keep our peace,

To the true uprisings within us,

For the slight raucous protest does not portray,

The true strength we possess beneath us.

Stand if we did, a stance if we took,

You will certainly know the beast rising in us,

From long built-up torture and unjust pain,

You disturb a monstrous giant sleeping within us.

We only want to live, as a free being should,

Yet you deem not, this freedom be given us,

You abuse your power, taunt and kill us for fun,

Without an inkling of remorse to receive thus.

Must this be, the one and only path,

A death sentence by those who cruelly hate us?

Where do we put our hope and trust to rely?

To gain the satisfaction to satiate us?

Our trust now lies in the embedded hope,

Of freedom given by the One who promised us,

True freedom, that cannot be taken away,

Out of Bondage, Set free, He will make us.

Out of Bondage, Brought home, He will take us.

Out of Bondage, We are strong, They will never break us.

Out of Bondage, We are not alone, He will never forsake us.

The Argument for Death (A Sonnet for Acceptance)

Can you enumerate the cost of death?

It's power over us now deeply holds,

Or take in the meaning for the last breath?

Countless from time immemorial folds?

What is life, we seek for reason to cast,

A hidden meaning for our mental pain,

A celebration of the forlorn past?

To fight to change the mistakes of our gain?

What is death, a constant separation,

A painful divide of our loved ones yet?

To miss that which once was in duration,

Its purpose, designed for human regret?

Nay, we must accept the final fullbring,
Our loved ones, no longer, are suffering.

Poems by My Mother

Good News

If I could spread the news from up above,

I'll tell everyone I meet, that God is love.

First, I'll ask those around, their point of view,

And let them know there's one, whose love is true.

I'll tell them the good news about our beloved
Christ

Reaffirming that yes! He paid the ultimate price.

I'll ask God to give me the courage to go to every
home and hut

And listen to everyone's stories, no if's, and's, or
but's.

Then we can agree, this realization makes the cut,

Sin, with its unhappy state, has us all in a rut.

But I'll tell them to take heart, that there's good news,

I pray that they would listen to my point of view's.

Our Savior Jesus Christ, The Lord bore all our sin,

He carried the whole lot; we can have peace from within!

I'll ask God to help me remind those who have forgotten,

that Jesus lived among mankind, yes, Christ the only-begotten.

I'll tell them, he died for you and he died for me,

And tell them again, we have the chance to live sin-free.

His love was destined to us from the start,

So this is what we should let abide in our heart,

And ask him for grace to let our hate depart.

Then we can move to action, we can all play a part.

Then we will be one, and all in unity,

And soon it will spread, throughout the
community,
Yes, it will travel to every city and every dome
To every capital city, every country we roam.

Love can change the world, it's the one principal
thing
Just think of how much our hearts will sing
Yes, I'll ask God to help me in my neighborly walk,
To give me a voice and I'll talk and I'll talk.
Jesus loves us all, our joy has begun,
For on the cross, the victory was won.
I'll ask God to send all help from above
for if I could, I'll start with Jesus and his love

I'll tell them the good news, to one and to all
He will give us his spirit, his power he'll install,
And then the latter rain will soon come to fall,
and all voices will be lifted up to give the last call.

Let's all be ready, Jesus is coming again,

Oh, love, his love! what sweet refrain.

A gift to us, the only thing that can change the
world again.

Let love fall upon our hearts, let love in its fullness
reign.

Yes, if I could change the world through love for
you,

I'll tell you what I'll say, I'll tell you what I'll do.

I'll tell them and tell them again; God's love is true.

This is my good news today, my good news to you.

Jesus Is Our Hope (An Explanation)

As we await Jesus' coming, with great anticipation,

We must now ask for grace to let go of all sinful gratification.

For the Lord, he is God, and he has paid for our Salvation

This poem is a message, a brief explanation.

When we are tempted to do things with a bad intention,

Let us look at the word of God, we must pay strict attention.

Jesus came to the earth to give us a sweet redemption.

So that the second death for us will be an exemption.

Let us by his grace, turn away from sin and degradation

For Jesus in his mercy gave us full justification

He also granted us his precious sanctification

And with his blood, he gave us a purification.

Let us keep away from all forms of fornication

And look to the Lord for Emancipation

The Lord, He is God, and he looks down on his congregation

Let us ask for grace in our life's travels to meet our destination,

And to help us with our sinful inclination.

So that he can keep us from utter destruction and devastation.

Come now let us pray for God's Rejuvenation.

For those who do not love and accept Him; this is a serious consternation,

Without him as their personal savior, working to salvation.

For when Jesus comes, he will have books filled with full names and no abbreviations.

Each person's name will have the proper pronunciation.

Then the Angels will be dispatched for the great mobilization,

Those who have died will be raised with their Godly certification.

And those who are alive will be caught up in this great transportation.

So let us end this with this wonderful annotation,

For when Jesus comes again, there will be a great celebration.

And indeed, a wonderful Coronation.

Part III

Author's Notes

Author's Notes (Short Stories)

Midnight Camp Fire

I wrote *Midnight Camp Fire* over ten years ago, around January 2010. I was in school at the time, studying psychology, and what it meant to have power over people's minds. I then wanted to tell a story to ask the question: would people overcome what appeared to be allegiance to their leader for the avoidance of harm? Or will loyalty reign supreme? Midnight Camp Fire tries to answer that question, although morbidly so. The fire was used as a backdrop to the men's dark, gloomy environment, to interject energy and mystery to the story. Fire is a strange thing, is it not? It can certainly kill us easily, but at the same time, it can warm us up, all depending on how we use it. Same as with life, depending on how we do things, the very same actions we do can either harm or hurt us. While the fire is not the main point of the story, its rather heavy presence helps contrast the environment the boys found themselves in, and how they saw the fire compared to their lives, especially the main character.

Office Blues

I wrote *Office Blues* to expound on one thing, and one thing only: Madness. How do people who are afflicted with insanity see the World? How do they work out the decisions that appear to us as "crazy" or "insane" as something that is necessary and normal activities to be done? It then hit me. *People who are thus seen as crazy by us, do not themselves think that they are.* This seems fundamental to those of us who deem the mentally unwell by their way of thinking of course, but not to them. They may very well see *our* version of what we deem to be sane, as the thing that is crazy. The "sane" actions we take, may be the things that are simply disturbing to them. It is from this point of view that I wanted to write *Office Blues*. As for this story, I wanted to write it to give you a clear idea, that to our main character's eyes and perceptions, the people who see him as insane are the *truly* crazy ones. Irony anyone?

My Mother

My Mother is special, because, a lot of the events in it, are real, and based on my life. All parts of which, indeed happened. Certainly not the fiction part, as no one is currently capable of traveling through time, but all of the events our main character visited were events that occurred in my life. Thus, in this story, and only in this particular story, will I share personal events of my life. This story is dedicated to my actual mother, who passed away, at the time of my writing this, only seventeen months ago, and who I miss very much. She loved to read and write poetry. She always read a piece of poetry and when she was done, she would always exclaim "Beautiful!" after reading it. Many people also complimented her poetic compositional style as well.

The Black Awakening

Hmm. This story. Ok, so this is gonna be a long one. Please bear with me. Firstly, let me just say this: I got carried away. This is one of my longer stories. I usually try to keep my short stories to about five thousand words or shorter, as I prefer to start another part altogether than write a "long" short story. After all, wouldn't that somewhat defeat the purpose of the "short" aspect of the short story? However, this story was one that needed to be told from start to finish. I have strong feelings about this story, and of certainty, many a reader who cares about such things will too. I make no apologies for writing this story how I wrote it. I wanted to write this story with the results shown instantly upfront, of what *could* be. This story does not depict the struggle that may come from attempting these endeavors in real life, for I know nothing is ever that simple.

The idea behind *The Black Awakening,* was simply to give those of us in the Black ethnicity, a realistic (fictional or non-fictional, you choose) blueprint of sorts, of how we may fix the failings and shortcomings of our race. Do not get me wrong. I am not in any way, shape, or form a racist. I love and appreciate all races, and very much, my own. I love and respect all genders and all creeds. I just sometimes cry in my heart at the state of our race overall, especially since, I know it could be so much better. I took liberties to go to extremes, to once again, show what *could* be, if we just stopped doing some of the things we do.

Do I seek to say that only our race is guilty of the vices outlined in *The Black Awakening*? No. Of course not. All races and all people are guilty of the things that harm society and dehumanize us. Will doing all the things in my story fix everything? Certainly not. But we can never know if we never try. The real question is, are we collectively capable of doing half of what I propose in *The Black Awakening?* Well, for that I will let you decide.

For those of you who are of my race, but argue that this is an unfair representation of what the Black race is, you delude yourself. Every single one of the issues I addressed in this story rings true and is the hallmark of the majority of the Black race, not all of course, but a very high majority, especially in America, especially so, in the inner cities. I do not seek to shame our race, nor do I happily highlight the vices and failings that plague our race, but it is necessary for us to see. We cannot change what we simply do not know or thus know, but refuse to care about. Now, of course, there is abundant and tremendous good, and the contributions of the Black Race to the world is something all Black people can be proud of, for we drip of sheer talent in everything we do. We have immense registers of the heights we can attain to, most recently even, as President of the United States. And even then, it should not need to be said that I think all people in our race are bad. No race has that. Every race has good *and* bad people. Every race suffers from ailments and vices that destroy their overall culture.

All races. Hence, we must not overgeneralize. I ask you not to seek a mental loophole to be against this work. Read the thing again. In it, you can see that I do not overgeneralize, instead, I *collectivize.* I collectivize *together,* the actions of the whole race. There *is* a difference.

I truly wish this story was a true blueprint to reality, I truly do. I do not attempt to put our race down, nor do I seek to make light or fun, as you see that I am not. Not with this story. I also do not seek to put our race above any other race or ethnicity, nor will I ever do this. Never, in all my writing. My goal with this story is to simply focus, specifically on the Black race, and how things might be better if we tried. I mean, *truly tried.* While the title of the story is called *The Black Awakening,* it might as well be called by any other race *"awakening",* to improve the collective livelihood and lives for all races, as people can see this story as a blueprint to a better racial and social future for all, not just one particular race. I simply wish people to take a look and see, what we could be, what we could *attain* to. If you do not think that a race, *any race,* could attain to the heights shown in *The Black Awakening,* then you must ask yourself why you feel this way.

Putting aside any feelings of animosity or bias, please remember, this story is fiction, it is not real, but I really and truly wish that it was. After all, is this story not inspiring at least, as a dream, to what Black people, nay, all races could be? Ask yourself. Be honest.

The Speech of Animals

This story by far was my most fun to write. I always wanted to explore what the world would look like if animals were allowed to talk, and we, as humans, were now able to understand them. What would happen? What would they say? How would Humans react to what they said? All these questions I sought to answer in *The Speech of Animals*. The first part of this story was designed to contrast between a simple house cat and her human mother, and what was happening in the outside world. This story, in concept, is both scary, yet intriguing. On one hand, I would love to be able to talk to birds, and animals as they went about daily life. Can you imagine what the older species would say? Could you imagine what we could learn from Fish, swimming deep in the oceans? Or Wise, strong Elephants as they traversed the terrain? Or simply the minute machinations of the inner parts of the earth from insects and bugs

THE MANY MINDS OF ME

who creep and burrow deep within? Yet on the other hand, would we want to hear the raw truth of what they might think about us? How we have thus treated them so far? How we currently live and use the resources on this planet? I think this story should prove quite entertaining.

The Speech of Animals II

This story is the second part of *The Speech of Animals*. I ended up choosing to write another story to accompany the first one, as I felt there was still tons more that I could explore in relation to now having animals being able to communicate with us. In jotting down my initial ideas, it came to me. Sure, animals could now talk to us, but would humans *listen*? Would we accept the recommendations of animals to our way of life? I wanted to explore this concept further. How would this play out? How would it all come to an end? While I know the ending is quite sad, don't worry. Who knows, the story may not be over...

The Lesson

I'm gonna keep this one brief. This story was fun for me to write, and I enjoyed it a lot, but you know why I wrote this. I wanted to use science fiction, well rather, made up science fiction, to depict a simple concept that we cannot escape. We're gonna die if we don't stop abusing this planet. Also, just so you know, it's a real possibility that even if we were visited by Aliens, they may not even *like* us. Think about that.

The Line Between Black and White

This was one of my most engrossing story concepts. I set out to explore one amazing concept. *What if* Man was now able to cure all diseases? What would be the ramifications? How would it affect the environment? I actually got this idea a long time before the current climate of the Coronavirus. As a health care professional myself, I wondered many times what the scenario would look like if we no longer had disease. I got so deeply carried away in my writing on this one! For this story, I was able to inject some of my scientific knowledge to make it appear as realistic as possible. Certainly, this should be the point of every good story anyways. As I wrote, I knew what direction I wanted to go, but I first wanted to touch on some real-world consequences I thought would occur should we obtain this wish. While writing *The Line Between Black and White*, I wanted it to sound as existential as I could, taking into account the perils of humanity losing the extremely important, and irreplaceable process of photosynthesis, that is: the way plants make their food, and how they breathe, all in exchange for humanity's freedom from disease. Interesting concept no?

The Line Between Black and White II

Here, I continued the events of The Line Between Black and White as the story was far from over. Now devoid of its critical and delicate balance with plant life on earth, I wanted to show that we would quickly devolve into chaos if we *truly* lost our food supply. If you notice, this second part is half as long as the first part. In all honesty, while writing part one of this story, I feared I was getting too carried away, as I did with *The Black Awakening,* and that I might end up writing close to over several thousand words. So I deemed to end part one of *The Line Between Black and White* around a little over four thousand words.

Another reason I chose to stop writing part one, was because whilst reading it with a fresh set of eyes, my girlfriend complained that the story was thus too dark. She said it was becoming stressful. At first, I felt that that was a good thing because I wanted the reader to feel the existential crisis now looming on humanity and the hard (or easy) choice they would soon have to make. But I realized that it would be better to continue instead, in the direction where I wanted to go, forgoing the dark, gloomy storytelling I had initially planned to portray in part one. For part two, I concluded the story with a personal question. This question was designed to be as hard to answer as possible. After all, when faced with these choices in reality, would it be so simple to just choose one over the other? Is it always about the future? Or does the excruciating troubles of the present hold the real, life-changing decisional weight?

A Stranger's Visit

Do you believe in angels? If you are religiously minded, you most likely do. Every religion has some form of "herald" or "messenger" that their deity created to serve them. My story is written from my Christian beliefs that angels do exist. Now, it needs to be said, there is no evidence we have to suggest that fallen angels live amongst us, or are serving life sentences as human beings for their once heavenly betrayals. No. This story is, to my knowledge, purely fictional. I enjoyed writing it, as my mind sometimes wonder what it must be like for them. I, however, did not write this story along the vein of good angels. Rather, I wanted to explore the premise behind what a fallen angel may do, or how things may turn out for someone along his status. I think *A Stranger's Visit* is a good read, and a great twist for the reader, for what you initially perceive the situation to be, is simply not what it really is.

The Amazing Opportunity

As a first-time writer/self-publisher, I wrote this story as an expression of fear I constantly experienced as I began to think about publishing my work out to the world. Many a bright-eyed author believes, that he or she will be the next *"Hunger Games"* or the next *"Harry Potter and the Sorceror's Stone"* author, where dreams of money, fame, and fortune will come, once you publish your spectacularly written, in-depth world of fantasy. Or, perhaps you gain worldwide acclaim as you create the next *"Jason Bourne"* series. For me, I never felt I would be one of those lucky people to have their work treated thus. I instead feared heavily, and sometimes still do (all authors do, to an extent, I don't care how prolific or established you are) that my work would be stolen, or abused, with little to nothing I could do to stop it. This story serves as a warning. Do not be so quick to think that there would not be people out there seeking to take advantage of you, your writing, or your ideas. I care not to make money, or to become instantly famous (although, a few extra book sales can't hurt 'eh) but I fear above all else, the abuse or theft of my work. I never realized how much plagiarism meant to me until I finished my first manuscript and was set to publish my work. All I now cared about now was ensuring I had copyright rights to my work, and that the world knew that this was *my* work.

There are some who claim that it is "immature" or juvenile to think that people will thus steal your intellectual property. I do not think this is immature or juvenile at all. I have joined many a writing group, where sad, pained authors post that they sent out samples of their work to various people and publishers, only to see that work sitting on the shelves of a bookstore while searching for similar material to write on. This to me is the ultimate betrayal. The ultimate heartbreak.

Others posit that it is unprofessional to mention anything related to copyright. To them, I say kiss my rear. Is it unprofessional to want to ensure your work is protected and not misused by nefarious people or people, desperate to make money, repackaging your hard work, and selling it back for pennies on the dollar? Inquiring about protection for your work is seen as unprofessional? Then let me *stay* unprofessional. If a publisher is thus offended, good. I will self publish, as I am doing and will continue to do.

To all new writers and authors, I say this. Take the extra step to register the copyright to your work. If nothing, but for peace of mind. Do not think about the financial aspects of this. Do it solely because it is *your* work. Marketing and seeking sales may come after. Registering your copyright to your work comes first. I pray you heed my warning. Once you copyright your work, then, by all means, send it out to the world! Don't hold back! Get it to every willing eye. For me, I write, solely because I love to, and financial gain can come, but I do not seek it. It can present itself, but I do not demand it.

Figure out then, what is most important for you, but whatever it is, do not leave your work unprotected, or vulnerable to such characters as those in this story. Also please, my dear new upcoming writer, as one of you myself, I caution only to be careful of words of flattery and persuasion, in getting you to relinquish the rights of your work to others, for I do not sit here, telling you to do something, without going through the same experience. I was also once approached to give up the rights to one of my stories, with many of the same events of this story playing out exactly as I wrote it. Be careful my dear writing friends, have fun, never stop writing, but please, be careful. You may not perceive the writing world as nefarious, but I can assure you, fewer industries rival the sheer cutthroat nature and dishonest actors involved than the writing profession. Much more so, to independent, self-motivated, self-publishers who thus only dream, to share their thoughts with the world.

Author's Notes (Poems)

A Descent into Madness

Fear not, my dear reader, I have not lost my mind...at least, not yet. I will say this. There are many meanings I sought to portray in this poem. I pray you can empathize and feel some of them.

A Moment in Time

This poem was written for someone. Someone *special*.

Fearless

I actually wrote this poem back in 2007. I was currently studying in college, and for me, school was never difficult, but I watched my fellow classmates struggle to work and take care of their families and still pursue their studies as they aimed for a better life. I wrote this poem for them, and also for all those who struggle and work hard to attain their goals, as they *fearlessly* push on.

My Noble Intention

This is one of my favorite poems. This poem has gone through many, many variations until finally, I was satisfied with the emotion I wanted to portray.

I selected every word meticulously. This poem started as a simple four-line prayer for inspiration to write something worthwhile for my reader. But as I kept writing stories, I worried about the quality of the entire work; wondering how the finished product would turn out to be. I feared it would not be good enough. Yet, my overall goal was to release some of the thoughts in my mind out to the world. This poem has deep meaning to me, and it was never really finished until I completed the entire book.

Qualities of God

I wanted to write a poem to characterize some of, and this is grossly sub-par to even attempt to contain within a single poem, the immense *qualities* of God.

Things Could Be Much Worse

I think this was the longest poem I have ever written, but the most fun I ever had writing a poem. I truly enjoyed writing this one. Growing up, studying some of the more famous poets, Poe, Milton, Shakespeare, etc. I wanted to write an amusing tale of bad luck. The idea came to me one day as I was standing in the kitchen, and I think I was cleaning up some spoiled food, and it spilled all over the floor! I thought to myself, "Isn't this the worst?" And so this poem was born! :.)

I've Lost My Light

This poem is written for all those who have lost something of "*Light*" in their lives. For me, that light was my precious Mother.

Were You Not Once Young?

I had fun writing this poem as well. I think this poem is, as my mother would say: "Beautiful!" As the title suggests: *Were You Not Once Young?* was written for young people. But it can also apply to anyone, young or old, who is still young at heart. I wanted to use the themes of nature to help portray and provide a sense of wonderment and beauty, combined with the concept of *aesthetic appreciation*. It was written as a statement and a question, of which to proclaim to adults, who now that they are grown, forget the wonders of youth. Not only do they forget, but they also seek to stifle the joy of the youth who are now coming up in the world. To the wonderfully *young*, I wanted to compose a gentle answer of which to provide to the jaded adult, when they seek to hinder or change the way you seek to see and envision the world and the future.

Out of Bondage

The never-ending stream of brutality and unjust shootings and killings of people of my race. The unjust, unfair treatment we always endured, even from our days of slavery. It has never *really* changed. Only *metamorphosized* to adapt to modern-day culture. They know they cannot wrap actual chains around our necks and beat us in the public square with whips, no. Modern-day culture would not allow it. Society would not allow it. Yet injustice persists. I do not have high litigation power to change this, but I do have my words. And I will use them. I will write, and leave these words, to be preserved forever, in the human catalog of works.

Instead of the old chain around the neck, they use the *new chain*, which is the handcuff and the biased system, targeting minorities. Instead of the old, cruel whip, they use the *new whip*, which is the baton or the taser or pepper spray, or their favorite weapon of choice, the Gun. Then maybe, if all of these aren't preferable, or perhaps they tire of such mundane tools, then a good old-fashioned *knee to the neck* does just fine as well. Or perhaps ten of them may jump on your chest to depress your respiration, knowing full well this is to torture and murder you, all in the name of *public order*. Take your pick.

While I appreciate all who would read my words, if, in the course of reading this particular poem, you are offended, then too bad. I make NO apologies for this poem. None. We watch on as countless innocent lives are lost from incompetence, racist bias, and *pure evil*, clearly shown, right before our eyes. unashamed, and unabashed. Then, if such brave people should step forward to insist that these protocols and evil actions be condemned and abolished, some decry that it must be kept to maintain public order. Well, right until this inhumane treatment happens to one of *their own*.

Public lynching's still very much exist. Cruel, unjust, vigilante punishment still gets carried out, with no *true* justice for these crimes and actions. *Out of Bondage* is the most emotion I have ever put into a poem. At times, I was extremely angry while writing it, and there are passages in the poem that tell you that. At other times, I simply questioned *why*? Why are we treated thus? Did we come from another realm and are not a part of the *human* species? It must be, because clearly, our race did something that only the racist knows, but the rest of the world cannot identify as yet. But who knows, maybe this "mystery" transgression will be revealed once they achieve their goal of attempting to torture and kill every last one of us, *all because we have a different skin tone.*

The Argument for Death (A Sonnet for Acceptance)

This Sonnet is a song for acceptance of Death. Ultimately, we all die. We watch as our loved ones suffer through disease and pain and long to comfort them. Then we suffer another acute pang of anguish, as we see them pass on. However, we must accept it. We must also remember, that above all else, they are no longer suffering.

Good News and Jesus is Our Hope, An Explanation (Both written by my Mother)

My dear mother. She wrote poems over her whole life, many of which were sadly lost, as there was no way to digitally preserve writings in her time, and many poems, written on paper, whether through the circumstance of life or unfortunate events such as fire or destruction of property, was lost to us. I lament this, as it is sad to me. You can find works and words of people dating back centuries on end, but I can possess only a few literary works composed by my mother. Through unfortunate circumstances, I have no way to view old work written by her.

Had she been a well-known poet, her work might have been preserved, but who cares for an unknown lady writing poetry? Many write but never publish. How can the world know? I don't blame anyone, I merely lament. As some read this, perhaps they will say that this should have been *her* responsibility to preserve most of her writing. *Perhaps.* Or maybe I should have taken the effort myself collect as much of her work as possible when she was alive, placing more importance on preserving her words for when she passed. But who thinks this? Certainly, only a few. She wrote two religious poems later in her life as well, of which I have two, and I wanted to publish it with my work, solely to include her in my first book; a way of keeping her work *close* to mines, forever.

Part IV

List of Pre-Story Epigraphs
and Meanings Behind
Them

Preamble:

As you have come to see, I truly love to use Epigraphs! They create intrigue and anticipation. When you read them, you instantly get a feel of what the story will be. You then make a conscious decision to invest time in "seeing" the story out. All my Epigraphs came from, and were written by me! I didn't look up or take from anyone else's work. I think Epigraphs are so important to a story, yet they are so fun to come up with. Why use someone else's saying or quote? Nay! I say, create your own! A splendid epigraph is like introducing yourself in the most awesome way, making people want to know about you more, just from how you introduced yourself. Isn't that cool?

The Epigraphs

"A Beacon of Hope, yet a Symbol of Fear, Doth help the frozen cope, or cause Man to shed the tear?"

This Epigraph from *Midnight Camp Fire* was meant for you to think about the fire as it relates to the story. While the fire is not the main part of the story, I used it to build intrigue and contrast with personal reflection.

"The World has two types of people inside. People who know they are not all there, and people who haven't gotten there yet."

This Epigraph from *Office Blues* should tell you all you need to know about our main character, Zacry. Oh, in case you haven't figured it out, "Zacry" is an Anagram.

"There is simply no way to quantify the love of the sole female who carried you. Don't bother to compare it with anything else. This is a special gift, given to us by God Himself. A remnant parallel, to the love he has for us."

This Epigraph I created for *My Mother* is a simple statement and acknowledgment of this universal truth. Regardless of man or animal, a Mother's love is a powerful, unbreakable bond.

"It is time to Wake up, I say. Time to wake up, observe our surroundings, and really see. Truly see what has happened to us. What is still happening to us. Let us see what is become of us, then, let us fix it."

This Epigraph suits the nature and theme of *The Black Awakening*. I wanted it to be a sound off call or a rallying cry. I could have chosen the rhyme, but there was no place for that here. The target audience of this story needs to wake up. We all need to wake up indeed.

"What words in rhyme can reach the height of its peak? For Animals now Talk, Yes, now they can Speak."

Such a cute Epigraph to use for the *Speech of Animals*, right? I wanted to lay the foundation for the reader early on: Animals will be a'speakin. And you know what? We should all listen.

"Tis' the second tale, of the Animal's speech in Conjecture, A Lesson in Wisdom, for The Dog will now Lecture."

This is one of my favorite Epigraphs. In *The Speech of Animals II*, I wanted you to be prepared for the repeated spoken proclamations from our main character, The Dog. I also came up with this Epigraph, as my girlfriend, while reading the story pointed out: "This Dog sure is talking a lot!" When I reviewed the scope of speaking entitlement and endowment I had given the Dog, I realized that this was true, and I laughed and decided to make that aspect my Epigraph for this second part of the story.

"Is it so bizarre to think that per chance, and this is a maybe, for we cannot know for now, but maybe, just maybe, Aliens don't really want to be near us? After all, what do we really have to offer?"

This Epigraph is too amusing. I wrote it strictly to get you intrigued enough to read *The Lesson*. If you read this epigraph, you are almost guaranteed to want to read this story to see where I was going with it.

"This story was meant, to open the philosophical door, To the realm of a specific miracle, but be careful what you wish for."

This Epigraph is by far, the most intriguing of all the Epigraphs I came up with. *"The Line Between Black and White"* is a ficticious, but very serious story of one big "what-if". That Epigraph, combined with a title like that, should be like catnip to your mind! Lol! It was for me, and I wrote it!

"What decision will Man, move forward to face? Such a terrible fate to choose, for it is a choice between a rock and a hard place."

I know, I know. "a rock and a hard place" is soooo cliched and overused. But for this particular Epigraph, it works perfectly. It pretty much sums up *"The Line Between Black and White II"*.

"This tale of the Stranger is simply not what you may think. Read every line, interpret ahead, don't blink."

I had to go back to the rhyme for this Epigraph. In a sense, I wanted it to come off as a riddle, making you curious enough to want to read and explore the meaning behind *A Stranger's Visit*. In this case, the story doesn't have an alternate meaning, but it certainly has an unforeseen twist.

"A simple tale of a frightening look, of flattering words, of writing a book. Who, from lacking in knowledge may think they see, a fantasy of grandeur, an amazing opportunity."

This Epigraph deeply concerns me, for I know that this happens to many a naïve author, who trusts that the world of writing is as pristine and clean as a *freshly washed woman*. It is not. I wanted to let the reader know upfront, that this story would be a tale of nefarious and dubious affectation. I pray you enjoy this story, but also, that you take and remember the lesson therein.

Glossary of Made up Words

About'h – About.

A'curst – Accursed.

Assurs't – Assure.

Be'curst – Same or similar to Accursed.

Befors't – Before.

Durst – Dust.

Hearse – Your Butt, Your Bottom, Your Ass.

Homesturd'st – Homestead.

Hurst – Heart.

Inner-Wurst – Inner waist, your Inner groin, Testicles, Balls.

Nurs't – Nurse.

Sparecraft – Spare Spacecraft

Yearn'st – Yearned.

Epilogue: Until We Meet Again

I hope you enjoyed this, my first published book! I was truly excited to get my stories and poems out there to the world. I chose to self-publish my stories and poems as a collection, as I want people to see my stories together, not over stretches of time, or in some one-off magazine or blog, but right here. Right now. I feel this gives you, the reader, a better all-around picture of what was going through my mind.

While writing, I made it my only creed to write once I truly felt something. Something from my mind that needed to be put down into words, whether comically-wise or serious. This was my inspiration.

I plan to write more! I am not writing for money, or to gain riches. God has blessed me with a good career and a good job. I write for the sheer love of it, and to inspire and entertain the minds of people who would read my words, just as I was inspired by many an author past.

Now, I am also always open to any and all critics and criticisms, (or praise) and I would love to discuss insights and gain further knowledge from others who have done this before.

I truly hope you enjoyed!

Contact me anytime at kingsley.nurse1@gmail.com

May you be blessed until we can meet again.

Perhaps in Glee...

From my *mind* to yours,

-Kingsley